Inklings Book 2024

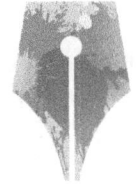

The following youth authors contributed their short stories and poems to this anthology:

Hollyn Alpert

Kyle Chinchio

Amaya Chugani

Henley Ferguson

Rose Ferver

Lola Grande

Mason Hong

Raya Ilieva

Kenzie Lam

Naomi Lam

Maya Mourshed

Tina Ramberg-Michael

Alex Rodriguez-Bader

Amrit Sivaramakrishnan

Khloe Ugarte

Penelope S.S. Wong

Archer Xiang

Eleanor Yue

Thank you to the following mentors for contributing editorial guidance and letters:

Kerry Aradhya

Jodi Anderson-Wolhaupter

Oriana Clapper

Rachel Delaney Craft

Betty Culley

Gina DeCiani

Erin Halden

Julia Hettiger

Avalon Felice Lee

Tasslyn Magnusson

Ann K. Morris

Lisa Frenkel Riddiough

Beth Spencewood

Melissa Uchiyama

Elizabeth Verdick

Ashley Walker

Cover illustrator: Naomi Kinsman

Editor: Naomi Kinsman

Copyeditor: Elizabeth Verdick

Printed in the USA

First printing: August 2024

ISBN: 978-1-956380-43-9

Contents

Foreword

Dear Reader,

The book you're holding in your hands is our sixteenth annual *Inklings Book*. What an adventure it has been, since 2008, to host the Inklings Book Contest! Each year, youth writers submit imaginative and heartfelt stories and poems for consideration. Our panel of judges has the very difficult task of choosing stand-out pieces from this spectacular collection of writing. Then, each selected author works with an author-mentor on a final editorial revision, collaborating to bring out the very best in their piece before publication. For most of our youth authors, the Inklings Book marks their debut publication. We are proud to celebrate their accomplishment alongside them, and to share their inspiring work with you.

Our focus in this book—in fact, our focus throughout the entire Inklings Book Contest—is revision. Lots of authors, regardless of their age, find revision challenging. Some even wonder: Is revision necessary? Why revise, if your work is already strong enough to win a contest? At Society of Young Inklings, our author-mentors have experienced for themselves the value of hearing an editor say, "I love your story. And here's an idea for how you might make it even stronger."

It's validating to discuss your creative writing with someone who cares about it as deeply as you do, a mentor who can help you ask: *What opportunities might we build upon in this piece?* In the interviews to come, you'll peek behind the scenes of our youth authors' revision process and hear about their discoveries as they looked at revision through the lens of: *What if...?*

If you find yourself inspired to try a revision of your own as you dig into this book, check out the "Dear Reader" letters from each author-mentor explaining the revision strategy chosen for their mentees for tips, tricks, and advice.

The authors featured in this book are in 3rd-8th grade. In their eighteen stories and poems you'll experience wonder, courage, surprise, and so much heart. Above all, you'll hear their passionate encouragement to you, to tap into your own powerful voice and share it with the world.

If you're interested in becoming an Inkling yourself, check out Society of Young Inklings at younginklings. org. While you're there, browse our membership and publishing opportunities, writing prompts, author interviews, and more.

Here's to you and your creativity!

Naomi Kinsman

Founder, Society of Young Inklings

An Enticing Opening

*Mason Hong worked with his mentor, Oriana Clapper, to refine the **enticing opening** in his story,* Aquaphobia.

Dear Reader,

You'll see in the upcoming pages that the very first word of Mason's story is *Crash!* With just one word, one sound, the story already intrigued me and made me wonder, *What's going to happen next?*

That is the reason why having an **enticing opening** in our writing is so important: it pulls readers into the story so they don't get distracted. And they continue reading as the story propels them forward.

Clearly, the beginning of Mason's story was already captivating, but in revision he added to it by describing the unique setting of the ship in vivid details, including the smells of the sea and the cozy feeling of the cabin below deck. Details like these immerse readers in the world of the story so they want to keep exploring further.

Mason also added a hint of the main character's feelings about the sea in the beginning. Throughout the story, Mason used a technique called *foreshadowing* to leave clues for the reader about what's to come. By hinting at protagonist Adam's fears in the beginning, when he eventually faces them near the end, our concern for Adam is much more intense, because we know that the obstacles he must overcome are so difficult for him.

When you're creating an enticing opening for your story, it can be helpful to ask questions like, *How do I want readers to feel when they start reading my story? And how do I want to introduce my characters and their world to readers?* Then you can play with the five senses, explore character thoughts and dialogue, and add little hints to get your readers wondering, *What's next?*

Happy Writing!
Oriana Clapper

Oriana Clapper earned her BA in Communication from Santa Clara University (and interned with the Society of Young Inklings) before moving to the East Coast to work in publishing at Hachette Book Group and HarperCollins for several years. Back in the Bay Area, she meets monthly with her writing group of ten years to continue to hone her craft for poetry and short stories. She lives in Sonoma County with her husband and her Australian Retriever, Scout.

Mason Hong

– Author Interview

Mason is a sixth grader at Taylor Middle School. He likes playing golf, trying out new video games, and watching football. His favorite football team is the Los Angeles Rams. He loves rocking out to AJR and Metallica on his electric guitar. Mason also enjoys reading fantasy and mystery books.

What changed when you revised for an enticing opening?

I just felt like a stronger beginning was going to draw more people in. I know that many authors have exciting openings, and I wanted that in my story. I managed to get it. Not only that but I also managed to bring in hyperbole, adjectives, and the senses.

What kinds of books do you like to read?

I often like to read fantasy, like the *Percy Jackson* series or the *Blackthorn Key* books. But I also like some good mystery books with characters like Sherlock Holmes or Charlie Thorne.

Why do you enjoy writing?

Well, writing lets me break free. Sometimes I just feel down, like if it's a rainy day. I write a short poem about a sunny day, and it just doesn't feel so rainy anymore. I don't have to be in the real world when I read a book. I could be in the story, forgetting about something bad that happened.

How do you come up with your ideas? What inspires you?

What I often do before writing is brainstorm, just spending ten minutes with absolutely no distractions. I let my mind wander to things that I often think of, such as fear, boats, or even school. Sometimes, I hit a dead end, and I start over. Not much really inspires me. Sometimes, random acts of courage and kindness give me inspiration. I just want to really build upon the first things that come to my mind and keep building on them.

What advice do you have for other Young Inklings who don't like revision very much?

Let's face it: revising is not fun. At all. You have to do punctuation, like that one comma you missed. But revising can be much more than that! Think of it this way: it's not really about cleaning up your room. It's more like adding better furniture to your room, like a four-poster bed or a TV. So, you don't have to think of it as a clean-up—think about revising as an add-on to your work.

Aquaphobia

by Mason Hong

*C*rash! The ship I was on, the *Turtle*, violently rocked, making me stumble and adding to my feeling of dread. The *Turtle* was a large fishing boat, decked out with beds, nets, and life jackets. While it was my home, it had never felt like a home. It always smelled of brine and copper. I was dreaming that I never had to get near the ocean again. The room was quite cozy, with dimly lit lamps and a beanbag I could sit in. Right before my stumble, the loudest clattering of wood crashing against the deck rang out throughout the ship, followed by some very colorful language.

Oh, great, I thought.

"Adam Welscy Bock, you come over here right now!" a voice above yelled.

I trudged upstairs, dropping the blanket around me that had I wrapped myself in, imagining my dreamland slowly waving good-bye. Above deck, my whole family, except for my dad who was on the wheel, stared at me as I sheepishly exited the stairs. Whenever I came up on deck, I made sure to look straight ahead and not into the water, because who knows what's down there?

Eyes straight, don't look at the water, look at the clock, it's 3 PM, eyes straight ahead, ohhh, I looked at the water, why did I have to look into the water!

A pile of wood planks were spilled out on the cold deck before my family. My mother was in front of my sister Patty, who was eighteen and a goth. I was only twelve, so she would always boss me around.

"You were supposed to tie the planks to the mast firmly, young man!" my mom yelled. "One of them almost hit me on the head! I could've died or gotten hit so hard that I could've forgotten that I was your mother! Do you think you can live without a mother? Now tie them up again!"

Sheesh, Mom, do you have to lay it on so thick? I thought.

Nothing was worse than your mom yelling at you and guilt-tripping you in front of your sibling. Especially when she was giving me that "You're in trouble" look.

I started to tie the planks while I grumbled under my breath. After the whole ordeal, I retired to my room. I hated my life. We always lived in the boat, only staying at most six months on land each year, so it was hard for me to make any friends. I mean, some days were nice and sunny, but the others were living heck, courtesy of storms, giant waves, and that one time flying fish came out of nowhere and bombarded our boat. I yearned for a normal life off this boat at times, and I'm sure that Patty had dreams of freedom, too. But us Bocks came from a long history of Admirals, Wreckers, and even pirates. So we had to do this stupid sea stuff. My dad made sure of it. Right now, the weather was nice and sunny out where we were somewhere in the Pacific Ocean but could turn sinister at any moment.

As I sat on my bed, Patty stomped her motorcycle boots down the stairs. I stared at her as she entered through the door, her black and neon green ponytail bobbing up and down.

"What do you want?" I sneered, with my pillow in my hands.

Patty walked over, her black lipstick slightly smeared and her dark clothing with some obnoxious rock band on her shirt somewhat wrinkled.

She sat down next to me on the bed, looking even more sad and angry at the world than usual. "Yo, ready for tomorrow?" she asked.

"I don't really know."

"Well, if you're scared, just follow Dad's lead. Also ..." Patty paused for a bit.

Great, another lecture?

"Dad's a little sick. Just watch out for him."

I froze. "Wait, what?"

"Mom didn't want to tell you, but I feel like you're old enough to know this now."

I stared at her in disbelief, trying to make sense of what she'd just said.

"But Dad hasn't had as much as a runny nose in five years!"

"I know, but he's been coughing more lately. Anyway, I gotta go help Mom prepare for tomorrow. Good night." She patted my shoulder as a gesture of assurance and exited the door.

"Wait, wh—"

But Patty was already up the stairs and out of earshot.

Everything will be okay. And Dad will be fine, I hope. I turned off the lights. The thought of Dad sick made it difficult to swallow, but I eventually fell asleep with a lump in my throat.

I woke up to some loud awful coughing, followed by my mom muttering to my dad. I checked the clock. It was only 3:00 AM. I kicked the sheets off, rolled out of bed and pressed my ear to my wall, hearing my parents because their room was right next to mine.

"C'mon Tom, you've been coughing a lot more lately," Mom said to Dad.

"Margret, Adam's Rite of Passage is tomorrow!"

I gulped in anxiety as I heard this. Our family's Rite of Passage was a test that was passed down from each generation of the Bock family history, each time a Bock turned twelve and a half. The test ensured that all Bocks were seaworthy individuals with skills to survive the sea, while also carrying the Bock name with pride. The rite involved diving to the *USS Taratong*, a battleship that once sank from a rogue wave many decades ago.

I was deathly afraid of the water, but my parents were never aware of this because I always worked on jobs that were below deck. I had never felt ready to undertake the Rite of Passage. I could not fathom diving into the ocean, much less facing what could await me in the depths of it all. There was no way that Mom would let Dad take me diving if he was sick.

"Fine," Mom said. "But once he completes it, do you promise you'll retire and watch your health and let our kids spread their wings?"

Hearing this made my heart sink.

Mom continued, "I mean, Patty wants to become an oceanographer who gives interesting speeches and teaches kids. And as for Adam, well, I don't know about Adam but I think he wants to do something else, something that involves more land and less water."

"But Mar—"

"Do you promise?"

"Okay, I promise," Dad said after a long pause.

"Good. Now let's go to sleep."

I trudged back to my bed. I spent the rest of the night dreading the next day, but my last thought before drifting off to sleep was, *Why's my father sick?*

A few hours later, I woke up, groggy and grumpy. I put my clothes on and stuck to my morning routine. When I climbed up the stairs, I was greeted by something so horrifying that I fell back down the stairs in sheer shock and hit my head.

"Adam! You okay?" I heard as the room spun. The horrifying thing was my dad, all wet and in scuba gear. This was a sight of my dad that I could never get used to. I was sprawled out at the bottom of the stairs as my dad exclaimed, "Guess what day it is!"

"Rite of Passage?" I said in an inquisitive tone.

"Yup! Put your gear on, I just checked the water this morning and it's great! Also, wear the suit that can go down to two hundred meters, it'll be a deep dive."

I stomped back up the stairs and into the dressing room, being careful to choose the deep dive suit and taking as much time as possible putting on one piece of gear at a time.

"Hurry up in there," Dad said with giddy excitement and in a hoarse voice from coughing.

Yeah, no. I'm not going to "Hurry up in here," I thought.

Once I had finally finished putting on my gear, I opened the door and waddled out of the room in my flippers. Right when I opened the door, a flash of yellow and white blinded me.

"Argh, my eyes!" I yelled.

My mother looked innocently behind her old film camera.

"*Aww*, you look so cute in a diving suit," Mom said.

Patty snickered behind her. As I flip-flopped over to the diving deck, careful not to trip over my flippers, my dad and I strapped on our underwater communication devices and tested our voice and speaker configurations.

"You know, *you're* going to do this to your kids too, one day," Patty said to me.

I only shot her a glare as she mimed taking a picture with the old photo camera.

My dad briefed me on what we were going to do. "Adam, we're diving to the *USS Taratong*. I'm going to let you in on our secret. I believe we are the only ones who know about this ship. Of course, the military should know, but you know about the Pentagon burning in 2046, around twenty-eight years ago, right?"

"Oh, *that*, of course I know," I said sarcastically. "Especially since I wasn't born yet."

My dad soldiered right past that comment. "Anyway, records of the *USS Taratong* sinking went up in flames with the Pentagon. Nobody really remembered the ship because it didn't fight in a single battle either, so we're the only people who know about it."

"Well, then how did *you* know about it, Dad?"

"My great-grandfather was the only one who survived the rogue wave that decimated the ship. I come here once every three years." My dad looked down for a moment, no doubt remembering the times he went down to pay his respects to his great-grandfather's fallen comrades.

"Ah, of course," I said. "No wonder why you always travel to Australia and then New Zealand every three years here in the Pacific, where the *Taratong* sank."

"Well I'm glad you figured that out. One last thing. There are sharks down there. They're all harmless. Except the bull, great white, and tiger sharks. Bulls are the worst but, thankfully, the rarest. If you see one, back away slowly. Very slowly. Okay, kiddo, let's go!"

My father coughed and dove into the water.

"Wait, what *shaahhh*—"

I tried to get ready to dive, but I tripped over my own flipper and plunged into the water. As I breathed in and out, I looked right into the depths. *Oh, no. I had to break my only rule. I have to. Look. Down.* I sweated, wanting to scream and return to the *Turtle*. I squirmed, sensing every blood-thirsty sea monster coming for me.

That's when something suddenly grabbed my arm.

Kraken! Loch Ness! Cthulhu! Shark! I tried to wriggle free, but the grasp was firm. As I looked at the thing holding me, I realized it was Dad. He looked into my eyes, his flashlight illuminating his features. His stare was comforting and showed that he was there for me.

"C'mon," he said.

I took a deep breath and dove deeper, following him. As I passed through the water, with my fears still ripe, my father led us deeper into the abyss, and soon we were at the bow of the *USS Taratong.*

"Over here!" My father motioned as I swam over, seeing a ghostly wreckage of a ship.

We entered the rusty hull of the giant ship, exploring the deck, damaged guns, and tons of aquatic life making the *Taratong* their home along the way.

What the heck? I thought. *The wildlife! The chains! The rust! Is this what Dad's life was like? Exploring caves and ghostly wreckages? I did not want this job. Eels swimming through the crevices, crabs scuttling across the floor … wait, is that a … skeleton?*

I sweated, feeling my fear of water overflowing as I stared hypnotically into the eye sockets of the skeleton, but I snapped out of it as my father motioned me to follow him.

Whoa … I thought. *Oh no, this is scary. Underwater skeletons all over the place! This is worse than I thought! I can't believe my dad does this kind of stuff.*

I saw my dad floating motionless next to a group of skeletons that appeared to be holding hands in a circle, likely making some type of prayer. My dad did the sign of the cross on his chest and placed a gold coin near the skeletons. Close to it was another pile of coins, probably from his other visits, and from prior Bock generations. Watching my dad made me realize that if it wasn't for them, I probably wouldn't be here, nor would my father.

My father looked at me and said, "Amazing, huh? I know you're deathly scared of water," he added in a somewhat soft voice.

I looked at him in surprise. "How did you know?"

"Son, we're your parents. We know everything, plus it's very obvious."

We passed the giant steel mast of the *Taratong* while he was talking. "Now, Adam, can I ask you, are you still afraid?"

I thought for a second. "No." Yet, I was lying.

"Good. Now let's get back—" My dad collapsed into a cough. I heard it and I knew it was bad, as I saw the bubbles forced out of his diving mask.

"Dad! Dad!" I frantically yelled. But he couldn't hear me. I shook him, but he was like a rag doll and did not respond.

The comforting bubble my dad had surrounded me with while diving suddenly popped. I was, as my dad liked to say it, in deep, deep, dookie. I panicked as I remembered Patty's words and my parent's conversation at 3:00 AM. *Dad's sick.*

My hands trembled as I tried to grab my dad's limp body. *Is it tuberculosis? Whooping cough? I am not meant for this job! I'm a deck swabber, not a doctor!*

I spun around, looking for anybody to help. But then I realized: I was alone. By myself. In deep waters. In a shipwreck. Trying to keep hold of my dad who might be dead.

I didn't ask for this! What do I do?! Dad, I can't do this! I can't do this! The thoughts came fast as tears clouded up my goggles. *If it wasn't for me, if it wasn't for the stupid tradition, Dad would be fine! Everything would be fine. But I have to do this. No. I can't cry now. I won't be able to see. Crying is for land. And I need to save my dad and bring him back to the* Turtle.

I was rudely interrupted by some object floating in front of me, but I couldn't see it clearly. I turned the flashlight on my head brighter.

In front of me was the meanest looking eel ever. It bared its teeth at me, no doubt trying to bite my fingers. I shrieked into my mask, bubbles erupting from it. I braced myself for the attack, but the eel just zoomed past my ear. *Phew!* After it left, I continued pulling my dad through the ghostly passage of the ship, trying to find a way out of the maze.

I finally got out of the ghostly wreckage of the ship when I suddenly heard an alarm: **Warning. Oxygen level is at twenty minutes.**

SHUT UP, ROBOTIC VOICE! I thought. *Umm, okay, think … think. So we have to take ten minutes to prevent the bends. So the* Taratong *is one hundred-eighty feet deep. We'd need two minutes at fifteen feet which left eight minutes to cover one hundred-sixty-five feet. So, we could ascend at around one minute every twenty-one feet. Alright, gotta go!*

I breathed, wondering how fast I could go with the heavy gear. With a grunt, I firmed up my grip on my dad's body and started swimming upward. As I came closer to the surface, I wondered if I could actually do this.

I breathed in and out, trying to keep calm and kicking my flippers as hard as I could when I finally saw sunlight peeking through the water. I believed that I could get to the surface. But blocking the light was a large silhouette, circling above us.

Oh, no … a bull shark.

I slowly tried to swim back to the ship, but the shark advanced on me, no doubt seeing Dad as a weakened animal—prey. And I was being hampered by Dad. There were two choices: one, I must stay with Dad and we both become chum; or two, I must let go of Dad and escape. I was suddenly wracked by the thought: *I don't know what to do, Dad! What do I do?*

I felt hopeless and helpless. Although, there was one more option …

My family and I were in the waiting room praying. My hands were joined with my sister and my mom. I led the prayer.

"Dear Lord, may You have mercy on us and our father. Please, let him survive, and may his health still be as strong after. In Your name, we pray. Amen."

I unclasped hands with my mom and Patty to see a tall white man with gloves and glasses.

"Are you the Bock family?" he asked our group.

"Yes," my mother answered for me.

"Come." He waved his hand over. We followed the doctor through the halls for a bit until we finally came to a door.

"Through here," the doctor said as he opened the door.

Inside was my dad, hooked up to an IV, in a hospital gown. I'd never seen him so … weak and helpless. It was heartbreaking. But in a little corner of the room, there was a heart monitor beeping, with zig-zags and "mountains" all over it. In the movies, that usually was a good sign.

"He's going steady. He's not going to wake up for a couple days, but he'll be fine. Your dad's going to be alright." The doctor put a comforting hand on my shoulder.

All I could do was break down and cry. My father, whom I had always looked up to, was going to be fine.

Twenty years later...

Avery woke, her blond hair spilling over her blue eyes as she sat up. She stretched and looked out the window of her room. The sky was gray, with some clouds. The ground ... there was no ground. The ocean stretched out from what Avery saw—infinity—and was nice and calm. She was about to yawn but was interrupted by her dad calling her from across the hallway.

"Avery Pearl, can you come over here?"

Avery put on her clothes, walked over to her father, and sat down on a plastic foldable chair.

"Yes?"

"I want to talk about something," her father said. "I know you're afraid of water."

"Yeah, so?" Avery recoiled because her father knew about her fear of water, even though she'd hidden it well.

"Can I tell you a story?" he asked.

Avery rolled her eyes. "Ugh, fine."

Avery's father took a deep breath and leaned in closer to her. "I was once your age—twelve years old—on this very ship, the *Turtle*. Before I went by Dad, or even Captain, I went by the name Adam Welscy Bock, and I once punched a bull shark in the nose ...

Sensory Language

*Amrit Sivaramakrishnan worked with her mentor, Kerry Aradhya, to expand the use of **sensory language** in Amrit's sound-driven story, Noise.*

Dear Reader,

Don't you love it when you read a story and feel like you're right there in it, connecting with the characters and everything they're going through? I know I do! Well, **sensory language** (words related to the five senses) is one technique writers use to make that reader experience possible.

Amrit's story, *Noise*, is about a girl named Sky who has sound sensitivity. For Amrit's revision, we decided to focus on language related to the sense of sound, since sound is so important to how Sky experiences the world around her.

Amrit worked very hard on her revisions, tackling them in two ways. One was to review her use of *onomatopoeia*—words that mimic sounds, like "crash" or "beep beep"—and decide if any changes could strengthen the reader's experience. We talked about how modifications to the words themselves, the rhythm of the words, or even the typography (for example, font size, capital letters, or italics) might make a difference.

The second approach Amrit took was to locate all the places in her manuscript where she used the word "noise" or "sound." I asked her to think about whether to keep each word as is, replace it with more detailed sensory language, or possibly delete it, if it wasn't necessary. In one spot, for instance, she ended up changing "whistling noise" to simply "whistling" in her final draft.

You might consider using these approaches when working on sensory language in your stories and poems, too. The second approach in particular will work for any of the senses—sight, sound, smell, taste, or touch. Try to envision what your character is experiencing in the moment to help guide you in choosing your sensory words. And most of all, have fun experimenting!

Happy Writing!
Kerry Aradhya

Kerry Aradhya is a collaborating artist with the Society of Young Inklings, and she loves playing with words and immersing herself in the creative process. She is the author of the picture book biography *Ernő Rubik and His Magic Cube* (Peachtree, 2024) and more than a dozen poems in children's magazines like *Ladybug* and *Highlights High Five*. Kerry also enjoys freelancing as a science editor and performing with a quirky modern dance ensemble in the San Francisco Bay Area, where she lives with her family and their cute but naughty pooch named Sofie.

Amrit Sivaramakrishnan

– Author Interview

Amrit is a ten-year-old member of the Society of Young Inklings. She lives in Atlanta and studies at the Westminster School of Atlanta. She is an avid reader, is a violist, and practices martial arts. She loves fantasy and mythology genres but enjoys realistic fiction from her favorite authors like Judy Blume, Kate DiCamillo, and Katherine Applegate. Amrit is a *Harry Potter* fan and loves to play "Hedwig's Theme" on her viola. She also likes chemistry, science, and graphic design. She loves Indian food and likes to travel to sunny beaches.

What inspired you to write this story?

The thing that inspired me to write this story was that I don't see a lot of people with disabilities and other physical disadvantages represented in books. So I wanted to show people what the people who have those disabilities experience in their lives.

What was your writing process like? Did the story come to you as you were writing, or did you plan it out beforehand?

The writing process for this story was very difficult for me because I experienced severe writer's block. To help with that, I planned out the story with a lot of diagrams and charts and idea webs to help me to have a good idea of where the story would go. Even though I did all of these things that could help me to overcome the block, I still had a hard time finishing the story!

Did anything about the revision process surprise you?

Yes, the revisions that my mentor gave me were very deep into the story and challenged me a lot. I had to work my way through the whole story and pick it apart thread by thread to make it better. My final draft is really, really different from my very first draft!

What was the most difficult part of the revision process?

Actually, the things that I felt were difficult about the process were the same things that I felt were surprising. It's because they were not expected, went very deep, and were detail oriented.

What has been your favorite part of your journey to publication and why?

My favorite part of my journey to publication has been working with my mentor to edit the story. I like problem solving, and going over the story and working with my mentor to edit it was like problem solving.

Many writers may be afraid to share their work, especially if they haven't been writing for very long. What would you say to those writers?

I would say, "Don't care what other people think about your story." It's great if the public likes it, but at the end of the day the only thing that matters is if *you* like your story and if you are happy with your story.

Is there anything I didn't ask you that you wish I had?

I would like people with disabilities like Sky to know that they are not alone. The people who don't have disabilities shouldn't treat people who do as if they are not equals or are lower than them.

Noise

by Amrit Sivaramakrishnan

*C*lank! Skyler felt the hard metal of her bright purple noise-canceling headphones press into the skin around her ears as she snapped them onto her head. The day's noise was too much, weighing her down with mounds and mounds of overloading crashes, beeps, and booms. She stepped into the noisy car, her eyes stinging. Her mom was playing music in the front seat, so Sky climbed quietly into the backseat, not wanting to add more to the cacophony raging in her ears. The hospital building faded away in the distance as they drove, but what the doctor had said didn't.

The words kept ringing in Sky's ears, *Sound Sensitivity, Sound Sensitivity*, adding to the pressure of the street hubbub outside. Her head felt like it would burst. She used to think she was normal like other teenagers, but she now knew she was not. *Hyperacusis*. That was what the doctor had diagnosed her with. The term made Sky shudder. Her ears were so overloaded, though, that she didn't have time to dwell on the thought. She was afraid that everyone at school, the neighbors, and her family would turn their backs on her if they found out about her diagnosis, thinking she was too weird.

Arriving home, Sky hopped out of the car, told her parents she wanted to check some books out at the library, and started to walk toward the bus stop, as usual.

She heard her father try to get her attention from the yard, calling, "Hey Sky, want me to drive you to the library? I'll take you somewhere afterwards! Hey! Sky!"

He snapped his fingers and made pleading faces, but that only made Sky more frustrated and mad. She couldn't risk enduring her metalhead dad's heavy-metal rock on full blast in the car. He didn't understand how hard it was to have sound sensitivity. Her dad didn't know how it felt to be surrounded by sounds that even the strongest of walls couldn't keep out. She *hated* noise.

The local public library was one of the only places where Sky could have peace and quiet, without the neighbors bustling by, or loud cars, or barking dogs, or anyone else other than her very best friends—the characters in her books. Sky stepped onto the sidewalk, hearing the out-of-tune orchestra that had been waiting to batter her ears. ***BAM! CRASH! HONK!*** She was startled at each new sound.

BARK! A dog distracted Sky from her thoughts. She refocused and began thinking about her parents. Before she had been diagnosed, they always thought the sensitivity she had to noise was just her being "stubborn." They pushed her to do things that exposed her to sounds, only let her read quietly for a certain amount of time each day, and never considered asking her how she felt about any of it. Whenever she tried to tell them about her sensitivities, they laughed and told her that they knew better than her. It was *infuriating.*

RING-RING-RING! The nearby bell of a bicycle made Sky jump. As Sky climbed onto the bus, she heard the harsh cacophony of familiar clamor she had to endure to reach the library.

Hisssss … The sound of the bus doors closing filled her ears.

VRRRRR! **HONK-HONK!** *Ahem!* ***Diiing!***

Sky shuddered, winced, and covered her ears but straightened her back and told herself to keep going. The bus was especially ear-rattling today because it was crammed. Sky could barely find a spot to squeeze into. She felt like giving up. Just one day with this new diagnosis, and she already felt mentally and emotionally crushed. She wanted to curl up in a ball, hide in a corner, and never ever come out.

"**ARRIVING AT THE LOCAL LIBRARY**!" the bus driver boomed through the loudspeaker.

Sky felt like her eardrums might burst. She stepped out of the bus and walked toward the front doors of the library. Inside, she removed her noise-canceling headphones and breathed in the scent of books. But the scent was tainted with the dejection from her diagnosis. Sky thought she might feel a little better if she could at least try to learn more about hyperacusis. She went to the nonfiction aisles and found a book about the topic. On the book's cover were the words, *Sound Sensitivity, All You Need to Know!* She quickly picked some random books from the how-to section so she could hide the book among them. To reward herself, she went to the fiction aisles and picked up the fifth *Harry Potter* book, her favorite, and then made a beeline for the self-checkout.

As she checked out her stack of books and bagged them, Sky was stopped by her favorite librarian. "Hey, Sky! Why are you in such a rush? Oh! You're reading a book about sound sensitivity?"

Startled by the sound of the librarian's sudden presence, Sky blurted out, "It's nothing! Just a school project!"

She quickly picked up her books and snapped her headphones on before running away. She was not ready to share her diagnosis with anyone. What if they saw her as a freak? Besides, talking to people and hearing their voices added to the pressure in her brain on a stressful day like today.

The return trip home was loud—again! Sky could hear a constant fierce whistling in her ears. By the time she reached home, she was very, very frazzled. She climbed the porch steps, wanting to go right to her room—

HONK!

Sky winced, clamped her hands over her headphone-covered ears, and quickly did a one hundred and eighty degree turn. A big moving truck was parked nearby. What was that doing there? She knew the quiet, elderly couple who'd lived across the street had moved away, but Sky's mom said the house was vacant. So, who was moving into it now? Sky was about to find out.

Just then, a teen girl came out of the front door of the house. She had olive skin and a pixie cut. She wore jeans, a black t-shirt, and sneakers, and she held some kind of electronic game. Sky saw her tilt it and twirl it, with an intense look of concentration on her face.

I wonder what it is? Sky thought to herself.

The girl tried and tried again, but a few minutes later, she collapsed onto one of the moving boxes, a look of defeat on her face. Sky realized the girl seemed sad and lonely.

A new girl? Right nearby? Almost exactly her age? This was an interesting coincidence. She had never really encountered other girls her age in her community.

Sky started to think about possibilities of friendship but immediately crushed them when she remembered her diagnosis from this morning. Even if she could work up the courage to talk to the girl, who would want to be friends with a sound-sensitive weirdo like Sky?

BEEEEEEP!!! CRASH!

The ruckus from the movers startled Sky, and she toppled against the porch railing. An intense ringing stung her ears as she righted herself and made her way to the front door with her (thankfully) intact bag of books. As soon as she set foot in the house, she heard her parents talking in the living room. Sky peeked around the wall, and her mom beckoned for her to come forward.

"I know this might be a shock after all that's happened today," Sky's mom murmured quietly, "but there's a new family moving in, and we're all going over tonight to have a housewarming party with them. I want you to attend, even if it hurts your ears to be at a loud event."

Sky felt a bubble of anger form in her chest. Her parents were again pushing her to get used to sounds, even when she had *just been diagnosed with sound sensitivity?!* They were so annoying and frustrating! Sky frowned. She didn't want to be pushed to familiarize herself with something that was painful to her.

I wish they'd try to have some empathy and talk to me and see what I need, she thought.

But she didn't have the energy to argue. Sky nodded mutely, turned away, and walked to her gaming room.

Her gaming room was Sky's sanctuary. Here was the *one* place where she actually *created* loud noise in the house. Sky had *EXTRA*-strong noise-canceling headphones for gaming. Somehow, gaming helped her to relax. Sky plopped down, switched out her set of headphones, and opened Minecraft on her gaming monitor.

As Sky played, she let the news of the day sink in. She couldn't help but wonder what it would be like to have a friend nearby. Should she make an effort at the party tonight? As Sky's mom often said, "There is no harm in trying." But was this true? What if making friends with the new girl was hard? Sky's mom *was* wrong sometimes (actually most of the time …) about how to deal with her sound sensitivity …

After dinner, Sky's parents said it was time to go to the party, but with NO HEADPHONES! Sky really didn't feel ready. Unable to wear her headphones to the party, Sky already felt like her ears were buzzing with unwanted chattering. Why should she have to expose herself to unfiltered noise?

She saw the look on her mom's face. *Disappointment. Disapproval.* Sky felt like a mess on the inside.

She gently pushed her mom forward, toward the new neighbors' house. "You guys go without me for now. I'll be there soon. I just need to think."

Her mom frowned. But Sky stayed firm. "It's *my* choice."

Sky plopped herself down on the porch and breathed a sigh of relief as her parents left. She could hear crickets outside. *Chirp-chirp! Chirp-chirp!* They were just loud enough to annoy her. Sky thought about her sound sensitivity and how alone she felt. What if other people, including the new girl, thought Sky was too different? And why wouldn't her own parents give her more support? Sky was glad she'd spoken up for herself and told her mom and dad to leave her be for a while.

As she sat quietly alone, Sky saw the new girl come out of her house and sit on her own porch. The girl looked lonely, tired, and sad. Maybe even a little bit impatient, as her feet tapped on the porch. Sky figured it must be a hard day for her new neighbor, moving all that stuff and not knowing anyone.

For a time, Sky and the girl kept to themselves, but then their eyes finally met. Sky felt the urge to wave hello. She gave a tentative wave, thinking that maybe the new girl didn't even have to know about Sky's diagnosis or her unpopularity at school. The girl looked surprised but smiled and waved back. Then, after a pause, the girl got up and walked toward Sky's porch.

"Hi, I'm Alex," she said. "I'm new here. What's your name?"

Startled by the sudden interaction, Sky blurted out her name, Alex's words still ringing in her ears.

"Oh, did I startle you? Sorry. I just want someone to talk to. It's so crowded at my house, and probably no one would listen to what I have to say anyway."

"You can sit if you want," Sky said stiffly.

As they sat beside each other, Sky felt awkward but then realized something. Alex felt as if her parents didn't listen to what she had to say. That sounded familiar! So, Alex felt the same as Sky did? Sky was always so frustrated hearing her parents say, "We only want what's best for you" but then would brush off her feelings and opinions. Her mom and dad focused on what *they* thought was right, without realizing the consequences for Sky.

Alex spoke up again. "Who do you live with? Were those your parents who came to my house earlier?"

"Yes," Sky mumbled.

"Do you have any friends around here?" asked Alex.

"No," Sky admitted.

"Oh." Alex paused. "Do you like origami?"

"No."

"Do you know how to play backgammon?"

"Yes."

"Do you like books?"

"Yes."

Sky knew she wasn't being social enough. But she just had so much on her mind!

Alex looked ready to give up and leave, but then asked another question. "What's your favorite thing to do for fun?"

"Gaming," Sky replied automatically.

Alex grinned and said, "Me too!"

Sky looked at Alex with new interest. Alex started to talk about her gaming experience, how she'd originally begun gaming, and what her favorite games were. Sky realized how much she and Alex really had in common. Sky felt her excitement growing. She started to participate in the conversation, happy to reply. Sky described her favorite game designs and plays. She spoke about how amazing it was that research developers could create such elaborate worlds within video games.

Sky asked, "Did your friends where you lived before you moved love gaming, too?"

Alex's face suddenly looked serious. She seemed to lose the spark inside her.

"My friends were gamers," said Alex. "But the time zone where I used to live is completely different, so now I barely get an hour to play with them at night."

"That's too bad," said Sky. "I hope you'll get to visit with them in person sometime soon."

"Thanks," said Alex, "but I don't think we will. Once I started getting ready to move here, my old friends and I started growing further apart. And now, we're just really far away."

Sky and Alex went silent.

HOOT! Pitter patter, pitter patter. CREAK! The cacophony in the street rang in Sky's ears. She felt bad for Alex, who'd had to leave her gamer friends, her hometown she probably loved, and all of the other things she held dear from there. Alex must be so lonely. Almost like Sky herself was.

Maybe Sky could do something to make Alex feel better?

Sky cleared her throat and said, "I think you've been through a lot, so I want to tell you something important."

"What is it?" Alex asked curiously.

"I went to a special doctor this morning, and I got diagnosed with something called hyperacusis," Sky mumbled in a rush of words.

"I didn't understand what you just said."

"I have hyperacusis!" Sky said firmly. Suddenly she felt more confident. "It's a hearing condition. I get really sensitive to sound. That makes it hard to do anything without my noise-canceling headphones on."

Alex nodded. "Thank you for telling me."

The words seemed to hang between them, but Sky was glad that she'd opened up. She reached out and touched Alex's hand. "I am so sorry about how you're separated from your friends," said Sky. "Just know that you're always welcome to share with me."

Sky relaxed into the quiet as the sun began to go down. She could hear the buzz of cicadas and the distant hoot of an owl.

Finally, Alex spoke. "Thank you, Sky. Do you want to come to the party at my house? I could use the company."

Sky agreed to go, and together they made their way across the street. Sky knew this was a big step for her, attending a loud party with a new friend.

Inside Alex's house, boxes were strewn everywhere and adults stood around talking and eating. Pop music played in the background. The noise rang in Sky's ears, the drum beating in her head, and the lead vocals leaving a trace of pain behind. Alex seemed to notice that Sky was uncomfortable and beckoned her toward the stairs.

Sky followed Alex into a light gray bedroom with a matching gray rug. The room had a vaulted ceiling and a white marble table with a crystal tray holding plants. A floating shelf was nailed above a chic white geometric bed. Best of all, there were three white tables placed on the center of the rug, with a gaming monitor on each one! Alex motioned for Sky to sit down wherever she liked. Sky chose a plush chair as Alex plopped down on the bed.

A crash from downstairs made Sky jump. *BOOM!* She winced at the ringing in her ears.

"Are you okay?" asked Alex.

Sky quickly said yes. But it wasn't true.

Alex looked doubtful. "Are you sure you're alright? You can tell me if you're uncomfortable, or if your ears hurt. I won't judge, *promise.*"

"Okay, okay, it's just that sudden sounds are a lot!" The words burst forth from Sky. "Noise pounds my ears like a battering ram! It's just so overwhelming. Sometimes I can't take it!!!"

"Wow, seems like you have a lot of feelings on this subject you need to let out," Alex exclaimed.

"I can't let my feelings show at home because my parents are so oppressive!" Sky admitted. "They keep pushing me to familiarize myself with all sorts of noise so I can handle it better. And before I was diagnosed, they said I was 'being stubborn' and still forced me to do stuff that involved noise! They hardly ever listen to me!"

Alex stayed quiet and then put an arm around Sky's shoulders. The gesture comforted Sky. She felt her anger begin to melt away. The party noises were still bothersome, but maybe there was something Sky could do about it.

Sky turned to Alex for help. "Do you have any earplugs or noise-canceling headphones I could borrow?"

"I don't think so, but I do know one breathing exercise that may help," Alex replied. "I learned it to cope with moving so I could calm myself down."

"I'll try it," said Sky.

"Okay, first think of a happy memory. Then breathe in through your nose and out through your mouth slowly. Keep breathing deep while imagining what makes you happy," Alex said soothingly.

Sky thought about quiet places, the light silence that lifted the burden of carrying all the sounds she heard, and gaming. Her favorite memories! She breathed in and out, as Alex had recommended.

Sky realized she felt better. Having a friend made a difference.

"Thank you so much," said Sky. "That exercise helped. Alex, you should start a YouTube channel and call it *Mindfulness with Alex the Gamer*—it would be a big hit!" Sky joked.

Alex giggled and shook her head. "I'll stick to gaming. But thanks!" Sky and Alex decided they wanted to play video games together for a while, but Sky remembered she needed her special noise-canceling headphones to help her cope with the continuous clamor of the video games. Sky sighed and asked, "Well, what do you suppose I should do? I *can't* just listen to the music and noise at full blast!"

"I think we could start at, like, *really low volume*," Alex suggested.

Sky thought for a second and nodded. It would be a little different not really being able to hear the sound effects, but it would be worth it! They powered up the gaming monitors, and Alex turned down the volume. She gave Sky a thumbs up, and they began. By using Alex's strategy, Sky found she could game without her headphones!

Sky and Alex had so much fun, they almost didn't notice when their parents called them when the party ended. Sky was sad to leave, but she also knew she needed her quiet bed. Sky went downstairs with Alex.

"Thank you for having us over!" Sky said to Alex's mom, and then turned to Alex. "Thank you for being such a good friend." She again thanked Alex and her family for their hospitality, and with a hug to Alex, Sky went home to rest.

Alex and Sky had promised to see each other the next day.

Sky was walking to her house and listening to the outdoor noises. A few minutes later, Sky settled herself into bed, and for once, she enjoyed the noises outside.

Hoot-hoot! *Chirp-chirp.* **Squeak.**

She drifted off, fading into dreams of singing, and instruments, and NOISE!

Internal Conflict

*Naomi Lam worked with mentor, Jodi Anderson-Wolhaupter, on a final revision focused on increasing the main character's **internal conflict** in Naomi's story,* How to Fly Home.

Dear Reader,

A sword fight.
A championship jump shot at the buzzer.
A merciless mountain to climb.

All of these seem like obvious moments of conflict to spark a good story, but how does a writer reveal a character's internal struggles? How can words capture what's going on inside someone as they try to process complex emotions related to identity, family, and a place to belong? Such an internal tug-of-war is what Rowan finds himself confronting in Naomi's story, *How to Fly Home.* For her revision, Naomi focused on how dialogue and external objects could accentuate Rowan's **internal conflict** as he navigates two worlds to discover what it means to be at home, with himself and others.

Sometimes, to draw out a character's internal tension, the writer needs to draw out the scene. Two scenes of conflict emerged as opportunities for Naomi to play with adding dialogue. How would Rowan convince the Great Guardian to forgive him and how would he explain his complex "dragon" feelings to his family? Naomi added places where Rowan needs to grapple with words to articulate his uncertainties and evolving realizations. In fact, most of Chapter Eight is new dialogue and internal thoughts. Another instance of revision is in Chapter Nine when Rowan originally stated he told his family everything. Adding dialogue turned that part into a moment for Rowan to find the courage to speak these words: "Sometimes I feel . . . angry. Sad. Frustrated. It feels like there's a dragon inside of me because . . ." I pause for a moment. "There *is*."

Internal conflict can also be symbolized by external objects. The two worlds in Naomi's story depict how divided landscapes can echo the tension in a character's inner landscape. When reviewing her story, Naomi was surprised to discover that Rowan could play more of a role in fixing broken connections. In fact, a broken object becomes an opportunity to draw out more creative courage from Rowan, if he seizes the chance.

When you're aiming to reveal more internal tension or development in your characters, try taking

Naomi's approach. She turned "telling" sentences into "showing" sentences through dialogue, thoughts, and description between those words. Stretching out a scene allows a reader to feel the emotional build. Naomi also reread her story and found a way to use an object as a symbol for Rowan's growing self-understanding throughout the story. Worlds are not just confined to physical places; keep exploring your characters' internal realms, too.

Write on,
Jodi A-W

Jodi Anderson-Wolhaupter is a middle-school English teacher currently coaching other teachers. She is always looking for ways to empower students' voices through writing, which is why she enjoys volunteering with Young Inklings! Writing inspiration and collaboration can happen at any age in life, which is why Jodi's also enjoying the chance to create a children's book called *Keep Your Face to the Sun* with her eighty-year-old mom and an eighteen-year-old high school artist. Find your people and your passion and write on!

Naomi Lam

– Author Interview

Naomi is twelve years old and attends sixth grade at Hillview Middle School. She is passionate about the environment, nature, and animals. Her hobbies include reading and art, and she especially enjoys drawing dragons.

What is your favorite part in your story?

My favorite part is the epilogue because it ties everything together. I am also proud of the connection between the dragon and human worlds, which also shows how different kinds of people can also find ways to connect.

What surprised you when you started revising?

It was surprising to find out Rowan would be creating the new orb. It was an unexpected twist.

What was your favorite revision? Why?

A favorite revision was fixing the orb because it changed the story the most. It really became about making something new. Chapter Seven also explored how Rowan found the courage to reach out to the Great Guardian. I added dialogue and description to draw out the scene.

From this experience, what will you take with you for future writing projects?

I will look for the themes present throughout the book. In this story, connection and memories are important. They guide the characters.

What advice would you give to other young writers, especially middle schoolers?

When starting, write something you're passionate about. Write what you like. When revising, try to discover things you didn't see before. Also remember the importance of perseverance. I thought about what the story would be when it was finished to keep me going.

What are your future goals?

I like nature and art. I might write something about animals.

How to Fly Home

by Naomi Lam

Prologue

A long time ago, dragons and humans were at peace. They traveled freely between their worlds and interacted peacefully with each other. The rulers of the dragons and humans were the best of friends.

But not everything stayed perfect. As time went on, dragons and humans grew apart, their views and opinions changing. After one too many arguments, the human ruler destroyed two of three Sacred Orbs that had established the connection between their worlds. Although one Orb still remained, the portal grew weaker, only allowing some to enter.

Generations later, humans raised their children to bury their anger and focus on peace, so no one could enter the dragon world again. Meanwhile, the dragons put their wise leader in charge of guarding the Orb. They sealed the portal between the worlds with their fury. For hundreds of years, the two worlds remained separated.

But there were always going to be exceptions.

Chapter 1

I wake up to light streaming in through the curtains. It's winter break, so I don't have to worry about waking up early for school. I was never good at that anyway. Mornings do not agree with me.

Slowly, I roll out of bed and take my notebook from my drawer. The worn leather cover is printed with gold words: *Property of Rowan.* That's me. Rowan.

I open it, flip to a blank page, and take out my pencil. I sketch a dragon down the side of the page. Ever since I learned I could transform into a dragon last year, that's all my mind can think about. I used to draw nature and write poems. I still can, but now my notebook is filled with scales and wings. I twist my silver dragon bracelet, a gift from my best friend, Luna, around my wrist. I always suspected she'd known about the dragons long before I did. After all, she's much more of a dragon than I am—bold, brave, and clever.

"Rowan! Fin!" my mom calls from downstairs. "Time for breakfast."

My sister comes out from the room next to mine. Her real name is Finlee, but we call her Fin. We head to the kitchen, where my dad is cooking an omelet. Slices of avocado toast are on a plate at the table.

"Thanks," I say to my parents.

They love cooking for us. My mom used to run a bakery, and she makes the *best* baked goods.

We have a good life, almost perfect. It makes me feel guilty when sadness aches and anger bubbles beneath the surface, threatening to emerge.

Chapter 2

Sometime during the first week of break, Mom calls us together for a family meeting. "Your dad and I have reached an important decision. We're all moving to California."

"Why?" Finlee asks. "We're doing fine here."

We live in Montana right now, and Finlee's right. It's nice here, with mountains and trees and meadows nearby. We're comfortable in our home.

"There's an opportunity for me to get a degree there," Dad says. "Following my dreams."

Dad has been working some simple jobs to make money, but his wish has always been to become a marine biologist.

"And your mother has found a good job there," he continues. "You know her bakery closed last month."

"We can't move!" I exclaim. This is a special place, where I grew up.

"Rowan, think about it. This will benefit all of us," Mom says.

"But … this place is so special. Remember all the things we've done here?" But I know my words won't convince them.

"It's just a house, Rowan," Finlee says. She seems to accept that we're going to move. "You'll get used to it eventually."

My mind is swirling. I know my parents have reasons for the move, but none of this seems to matter now. Luna lived here before she … disappeared a year ago. Now there's no chance I'll ever see her again. I think of all the memories I've made here … like the treehouse in the backyard our family built together, the solar system painting on our ceiling.

"I don't care!" I yell. "*You* don't care. You're all so selfish!"

The dragon inside me is roaring, trying to get out. It's too overwhelming, and before I can think, I run outside into the forest.

Something is guiding me as I dodge trees and roots. Pulling me toward some mysterious place. And eventually, I find it: a small, clear pool and next to it, a gold plaque carved with a dragon shape.

What is this? I think. *Is it related to dragons?*

Usually, once I calm down, the dragon feeling goes away, but this time, it doesn't. The pool—*or maybe portal*—seems to make the feeling stronger. After weighing the possibilities in my mind, I take a deep breath and jump in.

Chapter 3

I expect to feel cold, wet water, but as I fall, it's almost as if a soft veil is surrounding me. For a panicked moment, I wonder if I've possibly died. But soon there is a solid surface beneath my feet, steadying my ground and my thoughts. I open my eyes in this new world. I gasp. I'm at the base of a beautiful mountain, with birch trees and marbled white and gray stone. Right in front of me is a stone tablet with glowing words: *WELCOME TO CALLIS ISLE.* That must be the name of this place.

I glance down at my watch, but it's not there anymore. Instead, scales have taken its place. I gasp.

I'm a dragon.

I've shifted a couple times before but certainly not fully. I have tan colored scales, with teal-green talons and wings, and dark orange spines down my back.

I tap on the stone tablet cautiously, and the words change to a map of the dragon world, with the mountain in the middle, and different circles showing dragon family caves. The map shows me that this whole area is a floating sky island, with others surrounding it. I can see the blurry edge of the land if I look hard enough. I look at the map again, and it's not long before I spot my last name labeling one of the circles: *Aeras*. In the long list of tiny names, this one sticks out.

Like a dragon in a sea of normal middle schoolers, I think. I trace one talon around the circle. *That's my family. They're related to me, even if I haven't met them before.*

Their cave is pretty close to here, and I'm preparing to leave when I spot Luna's family name.

My thoughts cascade like water. *What if she's here? If she is, why didn't she come back? What if I can't go back?* But I shake off the doubt. *Time to try out flying.*

At first, I rise unsteadily, awkwardly flapping my wings; but soon, I guess my dragon instincts kick in, because I'm swiftly flying. Before I'm quite ready, I'm in front of a large wooden door in a cliffside, starting to reconsider my choices. Not sure what to do next, I knock on the door. A moment later, the door opens and I'm greeted by a black and brown dragon.

"Hi," I say nervously.

The thought that this dragon is related to me is shocking.

"Greetings," the dragon says. His voice is low and growly. "Who are you?"

Then he tilts his head, as if looking at me sideways will make him suddenly understand.

"Um, Rowan Aeras. I think I'm supposed to be related to you?"

"Oh, wonderful! I'm Nightjar. You can call me Night," Nightjar says. "Let me check our family book. You can come in."

He opens a heavy door and steps into a giant house. I linger outside the door, searching inside for other dragons. I see a few at a table, who seem to be playing a kind of game with wooden pieces.

"*Hmm*, where is it, where is it," Night mutters. "Oh, dear, sorry. The house is a mess. We don't usually get visitors."

"Uh, it's okay," I say.

"Found it!" Night returns with an ancient-looking, thick book. He flips through it for what seems like an eternity and finally looks up. "Here you are. Rowan Aeras?"

I nod.

Night flips around, and then his face lights up. "You're my grandson!"

"Cool," I say.

Nerves stop me from saying anything else. But on the inside, I'm a warm kind of happy. I've finally found the right dragons! My people—or dragons, I guess.

There's a moment of awkward silence, and then Night says, "Come in—let me introduce you to the rest."

My heart pounds as he calls, "Everyone! Come meet my grandson!"

Chapter 4

The dragons at the table get up, followed by another large group from somewhere inside the house. They're all different sizes and colors, and all of them talk at once.

"Hi!" A young purple and orange dragonling runs up to me. "Wow, I'm so excited to meet you. We must be siblings or cousins or something, 'cause I'm his granddaughter," she says, pointing a claw at Night. "Why haven't you been here before?" she asks me. "I haven't seen you around."

"I've been in, um, the human world. I just discovered the portal. So, this place is . . . Callis Isle?"

The dragonling nods. "My name is Canna. Nice to meet you!" She rushes away with her friends, laughing.

An odd blue-gray dragon brushes past me, and then stops. "A

human, aren't you?" they say. "I thought that wasn't possible, but times are changing. Just remember, choose wisely. You may be split between the worlds now, but it's almost your time for the Choosing." They turn and walk away, leaving me with many questions.

I find a quiet time and approach Night. "Night? What's the Choosing?" I'm hoping I'll get more answers.

"*Hmm* … well, at some point, you'll have to choose whether you want to be a dragon or human. Most of us don't have to choose, only the ones who've experienced both worlds. You will know when the time is right."

Being a dragon seems so much better. I'd miss my family, but … they never really understood me.

I feel guilty, but still, it seems … easier here.

"Why me? How come *I* found this place instead of other people?" I ask.

"We don't know, but it's probably related to your personality or actions, we think," says Night. "I'm sure the Great Guardian would know."

I nod absentmindedly, focused on something else. I had often joked that Luna had a dragon's personality. Maybe she's here?

"Sorry, I have somewhere to go," I say.

"Already? It hasn't been that long. Well, I can tell you have something important to do. I hope you come back here soon." Night waves as I leave his dragon home.

I really *do* want to find Luna. I located her family name on the map, and I can't wait any longer to find her.

It's not hard to locate her family's place, a short distance from my family's. I spot a marbled rock cave, with vines on the outside.

I approach the rocky shelter, but a sunset-colored dragon stops me. "Who are you?" she demands, blocking me with her wings.

I recognize that voice. I can hear my heart beating inside me, drowning out my thoughts. I'm not sure how this strange reunion will go.

It's *Luna.*

Chapter 5

S uddenly, she recognizes me too. "Rowan?" she asks, squinting. "What are you doing here?"

"I—I found the portal—why didn't you come back? I missed you so much!" I want to hug her, but I'm not sure we're still friends. We'd had a fight the last time I saw her, and so much time has passed.

"I missed you, too," she says, smiling slightly. "But once I came through the portal, I found that I couldn't go back. Eventually, I just got used to living here. And I have so much to show you!"

Luna beckons to me with her wing and lifts off, and I follow her. The island is beautiful, but Luna says the most amazing part is coming soon: the Orb of Life.

I pick up the Orb and stare at it as smoky images swirl across the surface. They tell a story. I'm immersed in the pictures, as they sharpen around the edges. I see dragons and humans together, then watch them fighting; I see portals and separation. Then I see my family. I'd recognize them in an instant. My grandparents, my parents, and us—me and Luna— in our dragon form. I gasp in surprise, and for a moment, I forget I'm holding the Orb.

Luna lunges for the Orb as it drops, but she's too late.

The golden glass shatters into small shards. I gasp and jump away from the sparks of magic.

"It's okay," says Luna. "I should've warned you. It's surprising at first."

"Is there any way we can fix the Orb?"

"I'm not sure, but I heard … somewhere, there's another island. The legend says that if we can find the Great Guardian, they can heal the orb."

Chapter 6

Luna and I stare out at the sky. A glowing golden line stretches from our island to the Sacred Island. The island has one enormous mountain in the middle, larger than the one here. The pinnacle is topped with green, and I can just barely see the Sacred Cave, radiating light. It doesn't seem that far, but I'm sure it'll take a while to fly there. We'll have to make a few stops on other islands.

Cold, sharp wind whips around my face and catches in my wings. I'm still not great at flying. The dragon world looks beautiful from here, and I can see a few other islands in the distance.

We can probably reach the mountain and come back in a few hours. I hope we can make it. If not ... I don't know what will happen, but it's probably not good.

We set off. For a while, all I hear are steady wingbeats and wind. And then we've made it.

We stop at the base of the mountain to rest, eating some dried meat and fruits that we packed. Up close, the mountain looks intimidating and elegant.

We're almost there. Maybe we can do this.

Chapter 7

As we fly to the top, Luna and I chat and catch up about our lives. I'd forgotten how fun it is to be with her. I make sure to hold tight to the bag holding the Orb fragments.

We slowly make our way up the mountain. We're so close to the top. Soon, we reach a flat ledge in front of a glowing cave draped with vines covering the entrance. We part the vine curtain and cautiously look inside.

There are no puzzles or mazes or traps. Only a dimly lit room at the back of the cave. Inside it is a stone pedestal, and the Great Guardian.

They give us a look of scrutiny and say, "You weren't born here, I can tell. I should have expected that the humans would come back. Why are you here?"

"I—um, we're here to fix the … Orb of Life?" My voice tilts up into a question.

The Great Guardian seems suspicious. I get the feeling they don't want to help us.

Can't you just solve the problem and get it over with? I want to say, but I don't. I need to be respectful and calm, like Mom always says.

I'm nervous, and I hope the Great Guardian will help us. I lower my gaze and hunch my shoulders, trying to make myself small. "Please forgive us, Great Guardian. Breaking the Orb was an accident."

Still, my apologies are empty. They don't mean anything.

I take a deep breath and ask a question: "Do you remember what it was like when there was peace? When humans and dragons were together? I'm not sure, but it must have been nice."

I notice a strange expression on the Great Guardian's face, like they are missing someone. Maybe I can convince them.

I continue to speak: "I'm sorry for what the humans have done to the dragons, and everything else that has happened. It's created a barrier. A rift between the worlds. But dragons and humans aren't really so different. We're almost the same, really. I think it's time for a new beginning. For all of us."

Chapter 8

The Great Guardian is deep in thought. "To fix the Orb would be ... hard. After all, it's a sacred object. Representing the connection between our worlds and everything that is important. It can't be fixed by just anyone."

I'm afraid of what the Great Guardian will say next. Is there no way to solve this problem? No way to heal the Orb and portal?

But to my surprise, they say something completely unexpected. "You two are different from the rest of us. Young, and part of both worlds. But for a new beginning, fixing the pieces is not merely enough. You must create something new."

Us? Really? I think. *This doesn't seem like something we'd be trusted with, especially after I broke the Orb in the first place.*

Although, what the Great Guardian has said makes sense. The dragon and human worlds should be connected again.

Luna and I look at each other. Even though we don't know what to do, I place my talon on a shallow divot on the stone pedestal. I feel Luna's warm scales above mine. Suddenly, there's a flash of light. We step back and watch as a new Orb grows. This time, on one side, it shows my family, friends, art—everything that's important to me. And the other side shows a new scene: a dragon and a human side by side. The start of a new peace.

But still, something lingers in my mind. I need to go back to my family. I don't know if I'll stay with them, but I should at least explain where I've been.

The portal near my house brought me to Callis Isle. If I want to go home, I'll have to return there.

Although the journey back is quick, it feels like forever. I step through the portal, this time back to the human world. Even though I've lived with them my whole life, I'm nervous to see my family.

I make my way out of the forest and to my house.

Chapter 9

Slowly, I turn the doorknob and step inside.

"Rowan!" My dad is the first to notice that I'm back. "Where were you? We've been searching everywhere!"

"You're grounded for eternity," my mom chimes in, but she's smiling.

"Lost track of time hunting dragons, huh?" Finlee jokes. "You're obsessed with them."

I almost laugh, but it's not funny. *Dragons.* Of course, she couldn't possibly know, but it's true. I've been thinking about dragons almost every day for a while.

For a moment, I stand there, silent. It would be so easy to say, "I lost track of time in the forest" or just say good-bye and go back to the dragon world but … that's not who I want to be. I need to tell them everything. And I do.

"Sometimes I feel … angry. Sad. Frustrated. It feels like there's a dragon inside of me because …" I pause for a moment. "There *is.* Today, I was in the dragon world. Even if you don't believe it, it's real. Humans and dragons have been separated for a long time, but I think you should know about it."

They're all surprised, as expected, and the house is filled with voices.

The hour afterward passes in a blur. I think they've forgiven me for running away. Mom says that she used to hear stories of the dragons but has never been to their world before. Mostly, my family has many questions.

Sure, they wonder about the dragon world, but most of all, they want to know if I like it better there. And I don't know what to answer.

Overwhelmed, I walk up the stairs to my room and sit on my bed to think.

Then, my surroundings fade. I'm at the portal again, but not really. It seems unreal, like a vision. On one side, I see the dragon world, and on the other, the human one.

I know what to do now.

I think about Luna. My relatives. How free it felt to soar above the clouds.

But I also think about my family. The memories that would stay even after we moved. My sister, my parents, my room.

My world.

I take a deep breath and step toward the human world and my family.

Epilogue

Life is … different now, to say the least. My dragon hasn't come back for a while, as if it was at peace now. My parents and Finlee don't quite understand, but they try. There's a feeling of openness between all of us that wasn't there before. They're helping me control my anger, and most of all, teaching me that there are no wrong feelings.

I have a new notebook, one filled with memories and experiences and dreams and everything I love. I flip to a new page but pause on one of my drawings. It's of my family and friends, dragons and humans, together. One of my best works.

My mind is filled with memories and thoughts. Humans and dragons. Together. I realized we had to be together to realize how similar we are and celebrate our differences. Mom, Dad, Luna, Night, and the others believed in my vision. They all helped me create a new Orb, this time for the human world. Both Sacred Orbs now show an image of a human and a dragon side by side, unchanging and solid.

Although our world is different, with no main sacred place, I knew just where to put the Orb. It's by the portal near my old house. It's still there, even after we moved, and I'm okay with that. I have a feeling that I'll still be able to find my way into the dragon world, no matter where I am. Now that the connection is stronger than ever, the portal is always open.

Luna chose to stay in the dragon world, to my slight disappointment, but I see her all the time, and she's happy there.

I'm happy, too. I think I chose right, staying as a human. I used to think I was so different, but maybe everyone is part dragon somewhere inside. Maybe all I had to do was accept that. No matter where in the world or what world we're in, I have a place to belong, people I belong with.

I learned how to fly home.

The Promise of the Story

Lola Grande revised her story, A Stronger One, *with her mentor, Erin Halden. They focused on* **the story's promise,** *or that feeling of satisfaction a story provides from beginning to end.*

Dear Reader,

You know that feeling when you pick up a book, read the description on the back, and you get all tingly with excitement? And you just HAVE to read this book about a girl who learns she can fly, or a boy who needs to solve the mystery of his missing family, or the best friends who stumble into a fairy ring ...

You flip the book open and start reading, and you're totally hooked. You settle in somewhere comfy, knowing it could be a while before you look up from the pages again.

Yeah, I love that feeling, too. It's because these stories are delivering on something we writers call the **promise of the story**.

At the beginning of a story, writers make a

promise to their readers about what kind of story they are about to read. An adventure story, a magical story, a mystery story. For example, let's say your story starts with a plane flying into a storm one minute and flying out of it the next—except everyone on the plane has disappeared without a trace! You're making a promise to your readers that by reading your story we will get to the bottom of this mystery.

When I first read Lola's story, *A Stronger One*, I was struck by her wonderful dialogue, her complex characters, and the rich, mysterious world she'd created. She also created a sense, in her opening pages, that something wasn't quite right about this village, and that I would get answers as I read the story. I was all in.

Lola definitely had a fascinating, twisty mystery at the heart of her powerful story, but the mystery wasn't always clear on the page. So we rolled up our sleeves and got to work, revising her story to make sure she was delivering on the promise of her story.

We started by making sure all the necessary seeds were planted in the opening pages. Lola and I talked about what her main character, Theo, knew about the village, his parents' work, and the beast attacks. And we talked about what he *didn't* know. Lola then went back to her opening pages and made sure that readers knew what Theo had been told, while dropping hints that he may not have been told the real story.

Next, we revisited the moment in the story where the truth is revealed. No spoilers here, I promise! But we did revise that moment to make sure that all the questions raised in the story had answers, thereby delivering on the promise of the story.

We all want to write stories that are satisfying to read. Delivering on your story promise is one way to do this. If you're working on a story, ask yourself, *What kind of story am I promising to tell my readers? Something magical? Something mysterious?* Then look to your opening pages and ask, *What seeds of magic, or of mystery, have I planted there?* As the pieces of your story come together, start answering those questions you have raised.

Happy Writing!
Erin Halden

Erin Halden got her first writing gig at age eight, when she named herself editor and sole reporter for *Spot News*, the daily newspaper on Jupiter. She's been writing ever since. She's a writer, developmental editor, and book coach who works with writers all day long. She lives in a one-hundred-fifteen-year-old house in Saint Paul, Minnesota, with her husband, three kids, and very nutty Labradoodle.

Lola Grande

– Author Interview

Lola Grande a sixth grader at Rosarian Academy in West Palm Beach. Other than writing, she enjoys drawing, hanging out with family and friends, and acting. Lola loves getting competitive against her siblings and mom while playing Nintendo games. She also enjoys playing chess with her dad. When Lola grows up, she hopes to become an executive producer.

What did you learn from the revision process on A Stronger One?
The revision process on *A Stronger One* allowed me to think about my story differently and answer questions my readers might have.

What advice might you have for other Young Inklings who might be thinking, *Hey, I don't need to revise!?*
I would tell them to have an open mind and to follow through with the process, because you might shock yourself and realize, *Hey, I kind of see why I needed to change this and add some thought here.*

What are your favorite books? Favorite authors? Favorite artists?
A couple of my favorite series are *Keeper of the Lost Cities* by Shannon Messenger, *Harry Potter* by J. K. Rowling, and *The Lunar Chronicles* by Marissa Meyer. I don't have a favorite author because I read different books from different authors. However, my favorite artist is Frida Kahlo, even though some of her artwork can be intense. I think her life story and her artistic abilities are incredible.

Are you working on a new story/new project?

Right now I'm writing an essay in my English class. We were asked to write about Ancient Greece, so I chose to write about the Underworld. I'm really enjoying writing it because it's such a unique topic and very interesting.

A Stronger One

by Lola Grande

I stare at the door, dreading what my mom might say.

There has just been so much on my mind right now I could use a supportive parent for once.

I take a breath and step in.

I smile.

"Good Morning," Mom says quietly without even looking in my direction.

I see her reading a book and taking notes for her meeting at her wooden desk in the corner. I pull myself together and walk toward her.

"Hey, Mom, I was just wondering if you think I have a chance of getting into the fighting crew," I say as I rest my back against the dark blue wallpaper with my arms crossed.

" … Sorry, what did you say?" she mutters, turning around in her chair and looking in my direction.

"Do you think I'll pass the test?"

"It's up to you to ensure that you do. However, if I were you I'd go get some breakfast and head to your last lesson." She turns back around and ignores me again.

I stop leaning on the wall and head to the door.

"Love you, Mom, see you tonight, thanks for the advice."

"*Mmhmm*, you'll be fine, Theo," she grumbles to herself, still focused on her work more than me.

"Thanks, Mom," I say as I grab the doorknob.

"*Mmhmm.*"

I shut the door behind me and let out the breath I'd been holding the entire time.

"Well, that could have gone better," I say out loud, without realizing.

I just wish she cared more about me than the dumb institute. Maybe if my parents weren't in charge there, they'd have more time to hang out with me—and care about me more.

But they have the institute.

All the institute does is ruin my life.

Should I really be complaining though? The institute saves lives, even though it is ruining my own. Innocent people are saved from the beast's monthly attacks.

Without the institute, hundreds would be dead.

I have to pass the test to become part of the fighting crew. If not, I could be killed trying, or at least that's what the villagers are told.

I walk a little longer and finally end up in the huge lobby. I go up to one of the many food stands, surrounded by sofas and little cafe tables near the doors that lead into the forest.

I see Riley standing near his crepe stand in his white shirt and tan-colored apron with chocolate stains all over it. His brown, floppy hair looks like he rolled out of bed with it that way, which he probably did without trying to fix it. His bright green eyes are filled with a kind of joy that forces you to be happy.

Riley is probably the only friend I have, even though he is two years older than me. The kids at the institute don't really like hanging out with me, knowing my parents will decide if they officially get into the fighting crew or not.

"Hey, Theo, what can I get you, buddy?" Riley says in an uplifting tone.

"You know the usual, a crepe with chocolate and strawberries," I answer.

"Are you excited for today?" He grabs the chocolate and starts spreading it on the crepe.

"Well … kind of. I mean, what happens if I don't get in? No one ever talks about the people who don't make it," I say, trying to keep my cool as I finally let out my concerns.

"Dude, don't worry, your parents will definitely make sure you get in. It makes your entire family look bad if you *don't* get in," Riley says as he puts the strawberries in the crepe and hands it to me.

"Thanks, Riley."

"Yeah, no biggie, you should have a lot more confidence in yourself, Theo. You're going to do great," Riley says, smiling.

I can tell he means it.

"I hope!" I say as I wave good-bye and run toward the entrance to the forest.

I open the door with one hand as I quickly eat the crepe. I sprint into the forest, dodging trees and bushes until I finally reach the armory. I see my dad helping the scouts get into their armor.

"There you are, Theo, you're late!" my dad yells in my direction. "I was going to start without you. Grab a weapon and padded armor for your arms!"

"Sorry!"

"Just grab your sword!" he says in a rush.

I grab my sword off the wooden stands hanging on the wall.

"Everyone grab your gear and meet me outside, and we will start your last lesson," Dad orders.

I quickly look around and see scouts running to grab breastplates and cuirasses, which protect your torso. Everyone seems excited but nervous, hoping just like me that they will be accepted.

This is our last test to prove we can protect our village and families from the beasts that surround our town. I *have* to be accepted—I have to do this for my grandpa who was killed by a beast.

I just don't want any more people to get hurt.

The beasts' attacks have lowered in number since my parents inherited the institute from my grandpa. I have to be a part of their success and help them stop the beasts.

I need to pass the test.

I just have to.

Before I get close to the other scouts, Dad stops me midway and gives me a stern look while saying, "Finally, you decide to grace us with your presence, after not only being late but also taking an awfully long time in the armory."

"Okay, okay, I get it, Dad!" I mutter.

I try to get closer to the scouts so he'll stop attacking me and maybe be a little more understanding, knowing I'm his son.

"Don't speak to me like that. Say, *Sorry, sir*," he says looking directly at me.

"I'm sorry," I say, rolling my eyes and looking down.

"You should treat me respectfully, Theo, maybe even more so because I am your dad!"

"Yes, sir!" I say loudly without meaning it.

As I walk over to the other scouts, I can hear Dad start his lesson, and I know his little outburst is finally over.

"Now, I will start my last lesson," he says, "which has nothing to do with fighting skills, but has everything to do with protecting our village. Don't protect it to impress me—have a *reason*. Now, all of you find an area to practice before your final test," Dad orders.

I'm the first to leave; as I wind my way through the trees, I can hear birds chirping. I can still smell the dew from the night before on the leaves. I look around to make sure no one is watching me, and I sit down.

How could he be so rude to his own son, and not even feel guilty? As I think, my eyes catch onto something sharp and flat reflecting the light from the sun into the sky. My gloved hands curiously touch the sharp piece of glass. I pull down my hood. I haven't seen what I look like in over a year. Once you're in the institute, you're not allowed to see yourself. Mirrors are strictly forbidden. Just before my eyes can look into the glass, I hear the crunching of leaves. In a shocked, panicked state, I frantically pull the cloak back over my head and leap up.

My heart starts pounding as I look up and see a girl with curly brown hair that frames her face perfectly and chestnut-colored eyes that match her hair and tan skin. She has on a red flannel shirt with a white tank top, brown pants, and black boots.

"*Watcha doin?*" she says with a slight smirk.

"*Ummm*, practicin—what do you mean, *What am I doing?* What are *you* doing? You're not even in the institute! You're not supposed to be in the forest," I say with a skeptical look.

"Oh, you know, just practicing my archery skills and I sort of got lost," she says with a carefree shrug, as she steps out from the trees a little more.

Only then do I notice she's had a bow the entire time.

"Oh," I whisper.

"Wait, you're in the institute, right?" she asks, fidgeting with her flannel shirt.

"Yep."

"Do you think it's possible you could get me in?"

"Not exactly sure if I can," I say.

Why didn't she just go to trials like everyone else?

"It's fine if you can't. I mean, the institute is kind of sketchy, anyway."

"What do you mean *sketchy*, and didn't you just ask about joining it?" I say, confused about why she would change her mind so quickly.

"I don't know, my mom says it's sketchy, and my dad thinks it's a wonderful place, so I don't really know how to feel about it at this point." Her eyes seem to lose the joy and excitement from before—they look even more sad and confused.

"Sorry, it's kind of out of place for me to be talking about the institute like this," she says shamefully, while kicking the dirt with her boots.

"No worries. Look, I've got to go. Maybe tomorrow we can talk, and maybe we can figure out how to help you get in," I say.

"Yeah, sure, sounds great," she says to me, gaining back that happiness she'd lost a second ago and smiling once again.

"See you tomorrow!"

"Bye!" I whisper back as I watch her skipping out of the clearing.

"Wait, what's your name, you never told me?" I say, stopping her mid skip.

"Luna!" she yells back, continuing her happy stride.

As I watch her skip away, I realize how weird she acted about the institute. She seemed like she was fighting what she was trying to believe, or better yet, who to believe.

Her Dad.

Or Mom.

I kick the shard of glass away, realizing I'd almost broken a rule—a rule that my parents would never have forgiven me for breaking. If it wasn't for Luna, I would have seen my reflection in the glass.

I quickly leave the clearing. I walk through the forest and find the scouts in a huddle.

The test has started.

I wake up to the sound of people crying and laughing. I sit up in bed and think back to the test yesterday. I thought I would never get into the institute; however, the test was so easy I had to have passed. I leap out of bed, realizing why people are crying and laughing—the results are out!

I grab a shirt, jeans, and slippers from my chest of drawers. As I sprint to the lobby, I think to myself:

Did I pass?

If I didn't, will my parents be disappointed?

How many people can pass and become part of the fighting crew?

I finally make it to the lobby, and everything seems to slow as I reach the glass doors that lead to the forest.

The results.

They are posted on the door!

I run over and take a peak.

In gold letters I see my name.

Theo

I passed!

A whole new feeling comes over me, as I see my name on the list of students who have become part of the fighting crew. I realize Riley was right all along: I would get in!

However, as I look around, I see scouts crying. I watch their tears roll down their faces, and I no longer feel as happy as I did a second ago. These scouts didn't pass.

I watch my parents come up to the group.

"For those of you who passed, congratulations!" Mom says, smiling. "Those of you who didn't, please follow your fighting instructor out the door to the forest," she adds, hinting something to my dad.

I see Dad give Mom a look of confirmation, and then he opens the door and walks out along with the group that failed.

"Now, the rest of you go about your day!" Mom says with a wave of her hand as she walks toward her office—pretending that the scouts who failed would be back.

I try to forget what just happened as I leave the list. But how can you forget the look your parents gave each other, or the scouts going to the forest? I might as well keep my word and talk to Luna. Maybe she'll be able to help me figure out what happened to the others. I run down the long hallway toward my sleeping quarters. I open the door to my room, which has windows that go from the ceiling to the floor. Near the window I see my satchel on the floor beside my armor. I quickly run over and grab the satchel. I take my slippers off and put on my black high-tops.

I run out of my room and sprint to the lobby. On the opposite side of the forest doors is a huge entrance that leads to the village. I pass the many sofas, scouts, and fighting crew members. I swing open the door and see Spanish-style houses and villagers.

I walk outside and see people buying things at markets and kids pretending to be soldiers fighting with sticks. I continue walking down the winding path, but I can't find Luna. As I walk, I hear a voice behind me.

"You passed me!"

I jump in fright. As I turn around, I'm face to face with Luna.

Luna is smiling, with dimples and all. I'm guessing she is quite pleased she was able to scare me, because she can't stop smirking.

"Thanks, Luna," I reply sarcastically, trying to control my voice from wavering.

I try to regain my composure as I lead her past a few markets selling pastries and bathing products.

"Look, Luna, I have to tell you something," I say as I see an empty space in the park.

"Yeah?" Luna answers, becoming more serious as she follows me to a bench.

"I got into the fighting crew. However, I'm not sure if I'm as happy as I thought I'd be," I say as I slouch on the bench.

"Why?" she asks me.

"Well, the people who didn't get in were taken into the forest," I say, watching the fountain in front of us.

"Isn't that where the beasts are?" says Luna, realization dawning on her face.

"Yep, that's what I'm afraid about." I sigh.

"Well . . . maybe the institute is lying."

"I can't believe that, though. That means my parents are lying, too."

"Are you close to them?" Luna asks me.

"Not really."

"Is there any way for you to figure out if there's a chance the institute isn't good?"

"Nah, not really," I grumble, trying to think of anything that could help.

"Wait, my face. We aren't allowed to see each other's faces in the institute. Maybe there is a reason why."

"That is so weird!"

"Should I try—"

"Of course you should!" Luna replies enthusiastically, as she grabs my arm and pulls me toward the water fountain.

I muster up the courage to take my cloak off. I grab the silk fabric and slowly pull it down. I try to be brave as I attempt to control my shallow breathing. My heart pounds so loudly I can hardly hear the fountain.

I allow my hands to unclasp the fabric as it falls.

I stare into the water, shocked to find a totally different person than I was a year ago.

My face looks as if someone took an eraser and wiped off half my face.

There is no way this is possible. My parents have been lying to me about the institute—about everything! The institute ruined my entire face!

"Yep, we were right," I hear Luna mumble to herself.

"Yeah," I say so quietly I can barely hear myself.

I continue to stare into the clear water and study my light brown hair and one blue eye that is still left. I wonder how I can still see, breathe, and eat as I always have, but maybe that's part of the magic of whatever has happened to me. Magic or no, I want answers. I need answers.

"Okay, that's it, snap out of it!" Luna yells at me. "If you want to fix this, you have to talk to your mom and dad."

"Okay," I say, pulling my cloak over my head.

"Go now!"

I sprint so fast toward the institute that it feels as if my legs aren't touching the ground. I keep running. I pass the kids playing soldiers and the vendors at the markets. I swing open the door to the institute and run toward my mom's office. I burst into the room without knocking.

"MOM!" I scream.

She practically falls out of her chair as she hears my voice.

"WHAT HAPPENED TO MY FACE? Why have you been lying? Not only you but Dad, too! I'm your son, why would you do this to me?" I scream with anger and hurt.

"No, it's not the way it looks, I have a reason!" Mom says, trying to defend herself as she quickly gets out of her chair.

"Really, then how do you explain my face?" I take my cloak off.

"The beasts won't attack our village if we give them the faces of kids. The cloaks take the faces over time. When we give the cloaks to the beasts, they leave the village. This is the only way to protect the villagers!" she explains in a rush. "The kids who don't pass the test are the ones who must take the cloaks to the beasts. Some kids don't make it back from the forest. By doing this, Theo, they save our village."

"What about my protection? You and Dad could care less about me!" I say as warm tears fall from my last eye.

"No, you're wrong. We tried to keep you alive by letting you pass the test! Your father and I might always be busy, but we will always protect you," Mom says, grabbing my hand in hers.

"Fine, then let me try and find a different way to pacify the beasts!"

"Fine!" Mom reluctantly lets go of my hand.

I can't believe she has been lying to me about the institute.

Everything we've ever been told is a lie.

I feel like running to my room and pretending nothing happened. I can't, though. I have to pacify the beasts and save our village.

I open the institute's door, heading for the forest, and see Luna.

"I'll help," she says.

"Let's find a beast!" I say with a newfound determination. I have to try to save the fighting crew and new scouts.

Luna and I run through the forest not caring if the branches rip our clothes.

"Over there, I see one!" Luna points.

The beast has a body like a human. Its face is gone; the skin ripples down its body like water. It has little claws that claw at the air, trying to find something to grab onto. It keeps crying out in pain as it bumps into a tree and falls to the ground, shaking.

"It's lost—it's lost, Luna," I say.

I watch Luna nod at me and tiptoe over to the beast. She places her hand on the beast's head. The beast's face twitches, and its skin turns from a gray color to a faint white. It seems almost as if Luna's harmless and protective touch has relaxed the beast.

"It doesn't need a face to feel safe. It just needs someone to appreciate it and care for it," says Luna, marveling at this discovery.

I walk toward Luna and the beast.

I rest my hand on the beast's skin and feel a burst of sadness rush through me.

"What do I do?" I ask Luna.

"Show the beast what you see."

I close my eye and think of the village, my parents, and the scouts in the halls.

The forest.

I have to imagine the forest.

I think of all the trees—the insects that cover the ground, the dew I see every morning. How the leaves turn colors every fall, changing the green forest into shades of brown and orange with hints of yellow. I try to include little details like the pine tree above the beast and Luna near it. I open my eye.

The beast's color changes from gray to a bright white that shines almost like a lighthouse, providing safety in the dark.

Luna's eyes stare into mine. "It worked," she says softly, as she strokes the skin of the beast.

It was almost like the beast just needed someone to explain to it where it was for it to stop attacking and screeching in pain.

It didn't need children's faces—it needed someone who could help it.

Now, at age fifteen, and after my experience with the beast, I work alongside Luna at the institute. It is no longer a place to learn how to fight the beasts that surround our village but a place where you can learn how to help them.

Mom and Dad no longer feel stressed. Instead, they hang out with me and are always asking me how I'm feeling. It used to be that the institute limited the amount of friends I had and affected my relationship with my parents.

The institute actually never ruined my life—it created a stronger one.

Tension

Khloe Ugarte worked with her mentor, Gina DeCiani, to the increase the **tension** *in Khloe's suspenseful story,* The Evidence.

Dear Reader,

Stories needn't contain fiery car crashes or stalking Dementors to make readers stay up too late to finish "just one more chapter." Even the quietest story has the potential to grip readers—as long as there is story **tension**.

Story tension happens because obstacles arise that prevent main characters from getting what they want. Tension is so important in the story because it creates anticipation and keeps your readers engaged. In other words, tension keeps your readers turning the pages. The first draft of Khloe's charming story sparkled, with a sympathetic character, Aimi, who lived with her grandfather after her parents died. As Khloe made clear to me, all Aimi wants is to know what happened to her parents, and the story is about her quest for answers. That's a premise with built-in tension!

For our revision, Khloe and I worked on building tension moment-by-moment. We wanted to ensure that the tension built from the first page through to the story climax. Our revision mainly focused on applying two tools. The first was playing around with the idea of a "ticking time bomb," and the second was to add layers to the relationship between Aimi and her grandfather, which would allow Khloe to keep her reader guessing about whether Grandpa was a good guy—or someone working against Aimi.

The "ticking time bomb" is a narrative device that builds tension. A clock (real or metaphorical) is set, and the main character has to act before time runs out or all is lost. The best example of a ticking time bomb can be found in Cinderella. Will she get home before the clock strikes midnight and her coach turns back into a pumpkin?

Knowing that a clock has started is key. Short time frames can enhance tension. Have you ever watched a baking competition on television—the kind where the host calls out, "Bakers, you have ten minutes"? The bakers start assembling barely cooled cake layers and mixing up ganache that inevitably curdles in some way, and the viewers start to wonder, How in the world is anyone ever going to finish with only ten minutes left? That ten-minute clock has started and as that clock ticks down, the tension mounts for the bakers AND the viewers.

Clocks and watches abound in Khloe's story, and

Aimi only has so much time before the doctor comes to see her in her room. On revision, Khloe worked to bring the idea of watching time through the presence of watches into her story, from the very first page. She also looked to make time frames shorter. Finally, she looked at whether she could frame the window of time remaining more clearly so that readers understood just what Aimi was up against.

Another revision avenue we explored was to add layers to her characterization of Aimi's grandfather. Khloe's favorite books are J. K. Rowling's *Harry Potter* stories and *The Wednesday Wars* by Gary Schmidt. Both books have characters—Snape and Mrs. Baker—that appear to be the main characters' adversaries but who turn out to actually be something else entirely. Rowling and Schmidt withheld information from the reader to keep readers guessing about the motivations of Snape and Mrs. Baker.

In revision, we focused on adding some internal dialogue for Aimi to reveal how she felt about her grandfather and his activities—and, in some ways, misdirect her reader. Khloe also figured out just what Aimi's grandfather's own goals were, but she withheld them until her big reveal came at the climax.

Khloe's story was fabulous when we started working together. By the end of her revision, however, she had created a nail-biter that kept me wanting to know more about the world she had created on the page.

I very much look forward to what Khloe writes next!

Happy Writing!
Gina DeCiani

Gina DeCiani is currently the General Counsel and Vice-President of a nonprofit association in Chicago, Illinois. Gina also has an MFA in Writing for Children and Young Adults, from Hamline University in St. Paul, Minnesota. Gina is the coauthor of two texts on professional ethics and has published articles as part of Forbes HR Council.

Khloe Ugarte

– Author Interview

Khloe Ugarte is currently a sixth grader at Rosarian Academy. When not writing, Khloe enjoys reading, cooking, and playing lacrosse. She was born and raised in West Palm Beach, Florida. Khloe has always had a passion for writing, so when her English teacher told her about the Society of Young Inklings competition, she jumped at the opportunity. She is so grateful to have the chance to publish her story.

What was the best part of the revision process?

I really liked focusing on the relationship between Aimi and her grandfather. I had wanted to make it feel more natural, and the revision process let me do that. I also really liked adding more details about timepieces.

What changed in your story after you completed the revision?

I got to add a lot more details about time, and I changed the birthday gift Grandpa gave Aimi so he gave her a new watch with the diary. That was all a lot of fun. I also said more about the relationship between Dr. Jeff and Aimi's mother, which helped show Dr. Jeff's reasons for caring about Aimi. That's why he is so focused on trying to control her.

What did you think when you got my email telling you that we would focus our revision on building tension moment-by-moment?
At first, I wasn't all that happy about this revision! That was mostly because I had no idea how to make changes to build tension. However, it was fun to learn about things like "ticking time bombs," so it all ended up being kind of fun.

What advice do you have for other Young Inklings who are thinking right now that they don't like revising?
During the revision process, make sure to focus on revising for one thing at a time. I first spent time on Aimi and her grandfather's relationship, and I added information about Dr. Jeff being in love with Aimi's mother. Then I went back to the beginning and added Aimi's new watch and used it to show that time was running out. It's way easier to make the changes this way.

The Evidence

by Khloe Ugarte

March 2, 2024

I woke up in a cold sweat in the middle of the night from a nightmare I had not had in years. The sight of my parents' car pulling away for the last time seemed embedded on the backs of my eyelids. When I finally blinked away the image, I saw a clumsily wrapped package sitting on the foot of my bed.

I ripped the package open and found this stupid diary below an antique watch. _So, Grandpa ... if you ever find this diary ... thanks a million! What a great birthday gift! I am too old for this ... I am thirteen!_ But I guess it was nice of him to think of me.

I might as well write in the diary; who knows what I might forget next. After all, I only had one memory from my life in New Orleans, and of course, it had to be the only one I wanted to forget. Grandpa kept saying it's "normal," that your brain wants to forget trauma, but I didn't think so. Imagine waking up every day, knowing there are parts of your life that you will never truly know about. I mean, I only used to see Grandpa at Christmas, and suddenly I was living with him. Talk about weird!

As for the watch ... it was no Apple watch, but there was something cool about it. It had ornate carvings of fiddles running along both sides of the body and seemed to be made of bronze. I flipped it over and found this: *To my dear Andrea, I hope this watch will last forever, just like our love.*

Huh … that was odd. I recognized the name, but I couldn't seem to put my finger on who this mysterious *Andrea* was.

March 3, 2024

Ugh … today was horrible! This morning, I woke up and ate breakfast as fast as I could to avoid awkward questions from Grandpa about his gift. I hurriedly grabbed my backpack and rushed to lock the apartment door when I heard Grandpa's bed creaking as he got up. I raced down the seven flights of stairs, since the elevator was always broken in our apartment building, and then began my twenty-minute walk to school, avoiding the bright yellow taxis that tried to get my attention. I HATE cars; I will never ride in one, ever again. Nothing my Grandpa says will ever change the fact that my parents died in a car crash last year.

I continued to walk along the cracked sidewalk, thinking about how I was going to perfect my jump-shot after school, when my best friend's shrill voice rang out, dripping in disgust, "Aimi, what is that?"

I looked down and, to my horror, I was holding Mr. Zoncles. Mr. Zoncles was a stuffed frog my parents had given me before the crash. I must have subconsciously grabbed him because of my nightmare. I didn't know what to do with him now, but I could feel the tears threatening to spill over.

I ran.

At least I think I did.

I don't remember how I got there, but I ended up at the park. I knew Grandpa would be so mad when I got home because I had skipped school, so I waited until the sun set (Grandpa's bedtime) to head back to the apartment.

Once I rounded the last corner, I noticed the light in the living room was still on. He knew.

I slowed my pace, trying to delay my punishment as much as possible. Each step was harder than the last, as if I was walking into a pool of quicksand. When I finally reached the apartment door, I took my time taking out my key and inserting it into the lock.

As soon as I walked in, Grandpa's harsh voice scolded, his words blending together, "What is *wrong* with you?!? You never skip school. Do you have any idea how worried I was when Mrs. Saurez called from school? *Preciosa*, never do that again! I didn't want to have to do this, but I think I must. You know I only want what's best for you. You are grounded. Give me your phone!"

I hated it when Grandpa was disappointed in me. I opened my mouth to say sorry, but before I got the word out, I somehow ended up in my room holding a weathered picture frame that used to hold a picture of my parents and me in front of our old house in New Orleans. But the photo was missing, and the glass was shattered. I checked my new watch, and it read: 11:27 PM. I rubbed my eyes, convinced I was seeing the time wrong. It was only 7:30 PM when I got home. I had no clue how so much time had passed since Grandpa yelled at me.

I heard a strange noise coming from the living room. When I walked in to investigate, I saw my Grandpa rocking slowly back and forth in his rocking chair, a look of contemplation on his face, the missing picture in his hand.

"You are cleaning the whole apartment this weekend," he said, his voice remarkably calm. "And after that you are going to go live with Miss Ranido for a while."

"What?" I shouted, even though I knew perfectly well what he meant.

Miss Ranido ran the local orphanage, and it was very overcrowded. Grandpa was going to give me away, but why?

I guess the real question was: what had I been doing from 7:30 PM until now?

March 4, 2024

I only had forty-eight hours to find some sort of clue to unlock my memories before any chance of that would be lost forever. So I cleaned the apartment as fast as I could, but with no luck remembering. When I finished the chore, I plopped down on the couch, exhausted and irritated.

"Um, Aimi . . ." Grandpa said, sounding slightly apprehensive.

"What!" I yelled.

I knew that was rude, but I was super angry, and all of my hard work had led to nothing.

"Did you clean the *attic*?" Grandpa asked.

"No," I said, trying my hardest to hide the smile that was threatening to give my plans away.

As soon as Grandpa had said attic, I thought of all the movies I'd seen where the lost treasure or magical lamp was found in the attic. I thought for sure I would find something in the attic to prod my memory. I walked over to the little chain on the ceiling that pulled down the ladder to the attic. I climbed up the ladder. When I spotted the plethora of dusty boxes waiting for me, I knew I wouldn't be able to finish cleaning before dinnertime.

It took me the rest of the afternoon to clean and sort through all the boxes. I picked up the last box, thinking I would never find the answers I was looking for. That was when I noticed the name *Andrea* scrawled in an untidy print on the side of the box. The pieces all started to fall together, and it finally clicked.

Andrea was my mom's name.

I don't know how I remembered her name, but when I saw it, the name just fit. My dad must have once given her the watch that Grandpa gave me, back when they were dating. I hurriedly opened the box, excited to uncover some lost memories, but when I opened it, nothing was inside. Well, nothing except a fine gold powder. I scooped some up and threw it into the air in exasperation. I was really hoping the box would explain everything, but then I realized the room was sinking—or maybe I was flying. Whatever it was, I loved it.

All of my worries and doubts melted away. I could feel a lazy grin spread across my face.

The effects of what I decided to call "fairy dust" still hadn't worn off later on. Grandpa seemed concerned about me, but he shouldn't have been. I'd never felt better.

March 5, 2024

I woke up this morning with a pounding headache, probably the aftermath of the fairy dust. Grandpa was talking on the phone, but his voice was grave, unlike the usual "I'm always right" tone he adopted after we had moved to Chicago.

I crept out of bed as quietly as I could, not wanting to alert Grandpa to my presence.

"… I know, Jeff, but she found the box. I can't send her away now. It's too dangerous. I'm really worried, can I make an appointment for one? Thanks, Jeff, you're the best!"

What did that mean? *Dangerous?* I guess it meant I wouldn't have to go to the orphanage. One thing was for certain: I was not looking forward to whatever that appointment was.

"Aimi, get up! We've got to go," Grandpa called.

It was time for the appointment.

I quickly slipped on a t-shirt and my favorite pair of jeans. I found Grandpa in his rocking chair, his hair mussed and glasses askew. I noticed he was holding his keys for a car he hadn't used in years. Panic swelled in my chest, my heart pounding so loud I was sure Grandpa could hear it.

"No," I whispered, the fear evident in my voice.

I was not getting in that car, ever.

"Look, *preciosa*," he said following my gaze to the keys, "I would not do this to you unless it was absolutely necessary. Don't you trust me? I only want to help."

Everything in me screamed *no*, but I slowly nodded. We walked to his rusty Mustang in silence, my legs trembling as I buckled the seatbelt. I could not believe that he would ever ask me to do this, even if I had not been very obedient lately.

I squeezed my eyes shut as the engine roared to life. I didn't open them until we pulled up to a dingy doctor's office at 12:30 PM.

"'Dr. Jeff's Emporium of Mysterious Maladies and Mishaps,' sounds super normal," I mumbled.

When we walked in, a strong smell of magnolias knocked me back a step, which was odd, because there was not a flower in sight. Grandpa talked to the lady at the front desk while I looked around the waiting room.

At first glance, the room looked normal enough: degrees and awards hung on the wall, there were neat rows of chairs, and stacks of magazines covered the tables. But upon closer inspection, I saw that the degrees were dated from hundreds of years into the future from weird places I'd never even heard of. What was even stranger was that the magazines had headlines like "New Record Set for Levitation Charm" and "Prodigy Sprouts Wings at an Early Age." How weird was that?

Before I could investigate further, an orderly came in and called, "Aimi Reyes."

Grandpa and I both stood up to follow him, but the orderly, whose nametag I saw read *Gerald*, motioned him to sit back down.

Gerald led me down a series of passageways that seemed like they would not have fit in such a small doctor's office, past a wing that read *Permanent Residents.*

"Um … Gerald," I said, "What's that?" I pointed toward the door that led to the wing. "I thought this place was just for visits." My brow furrowed with concern.

"Oh, those rooms are just for the tough nuts to crack," he responded, only adding to my bewilderment. "Come along then."

Gerald led me even further into the labyrinth, until we reached a door that read Dr. Jeff Tanning, the guy Grandpa had been on the phone with this morning.

"Alright, here we are. Dr. Jeff will be here in ten minutes."

"Wait!" I said as Gerald started to walk away. "What is this place?"

Gerald looked at me and then spoke, his voice full of pity. "Don't worry, it will all be over soon."

I checked my watch again, and it was only 12:40 PM. I could feel my heartbeat quickening with every tick of the second hand as Gerald began to walk away. All I could do was wait.

"Please help me!" I wailed, starting to get desperate.

It was too late. I could hear Gerald's footsteps receding, and when the light hit him as he passed a window, I swore I saw two glimmers of what I could only describe as wings near his shoulders.

I sat down in one of those stiff doctor's office chairs and noticed Gerald's name tag on the floor. I reached to pick it up, and my eyes immediately found the barcode underneath his photo. My thoughts wandered to the scanner I'd noticed outside the *Permanent Residents* wing.

Before my brain knew what I was doing, my feet took me to the door to the wing. I scanned the name tag, and miraculously, the door opened. For the second time, the smell of magnolias attacked my nostrils. It seemed oddly familiar to me, but I couldn't put my finger on why.

The sound of high heels clacking snapped me out of my trance. I practically leaped toward the closest door I could find.

Relief swelled in my chest but was quickly replaced by confusion because the room I'd entered was filled with nothing but clocks and watches of all shapes and sizes. They filled the room with an eerie tick that gave me a pounding headache and made me want to run all the way back home. I nervously fidgeted with Gerald's name tag, and to my surprise a folded slip of paper fell out of the top, reading:

> *The clock strikes one,*
> *It's time for you to run.*
> *Three less down the middle*
> *On the watch*
> *Shaped like a fiddle.*

A clue? I immediately looked down to the watch on my wrist, thinking the unimaginable. How on earth could my parents tie into all of this?

Gerald was on my side. He seemed to want to help me, but why did this clue have to be so cryptic? I figured *When the clock strikes one, it's time for you to run* meant that at 1:00 PM I had to go back to the room Gerald had assigned to me because Dr. Jeff would arrive. The next couple of lines of the clue might as well have been gibberish.

I started looking for a timepiece shaped like a fiddle, hoping my wristwatch had nothing to do with it. Just then, an especially ornate pocket watch caught my eye.

I turned this pocket watch in my hand and saw the inscription: *To my Jeff, I love you forever and always—Andrea* written in loopy letters.

"What the?" I whispered, feeling my eyebrows raise so high they were practically in my hair.

Did this mean my dad's name was Jeff? Was he still alive? None of this made sense. The name Jeff didn't ring a bell for me, like the name Andrea had. But who else would my mom have promised to love forever and always?

I began to fiddle with the pocket watch's chain, wondering what *Three less down the middle* had meant. Then the answer clicked. I had to shorten this chain!

I unlatched the top three links, wondering what that was supposed to do. I looked at the time: 12:50 PM. I knew I should probably head back to the room Gerald had put me in, but I could feel the secrets to my memory loss hidden within the walls of this wing. So, I continued to explore.

I entered room after room, avoiding the ones with names on the door because they might be offices or for the permanent residents. Then, I finally found what I was looking for: the filing room.

I made a beeline for the R-W cabinet. I found my file under Reyes and, to my surprise, I also found one that read *Andrea Reyes*. My mom's file. And it smelled of magnolias.

That was when the answer hit me—my mom had always worn perfume that smelled like that flower. Next to her file was one for *Thomas Reyes*, probably my dad. His name fit better than Jeff, but then who on earth was Jeff and why would my mom have engraved those words on a timepiece for him?

I opened my mom's file, my fingers shaking. This was it, the moment when I would finally get the truth.

Andrea Reyes

Gender: Female

Species: Fairy

Ailment/Reason Hospitalized: She was going to turn me in, so I had no other choice but to hospitalize her. Ever since we were little, we had dreamed of getting into the Academy. It was the best school of charm and magic at the time. When the time finally came, only one of us got in: Andrea. I knew this was only because of her father's connections; Mr. Chapman was always pulling strings, and I could not be bested by my fiancé. I would look ridiculous! I plotted my revenge and during that time Andrea got a new boyfriend, they married, and they raised a family. A few years later, I confronted her about it, and in my frustration, I told her my plans to expose our race to the world. I meant it as a threat, but she had already called the Patrol. I panicked and took her to my emporium in the human realm. At least then her daughter would be deported or even better, executed, because her parents were deemed dead. After all, fairies are supposed to live forever, so if one dies they and all their offspring are the imposters that the prophecy foretold.

Doctor Signature: *Dr. Jeff Tanning*

My head was spinning as I shoved all three files into my pocket. Looking at my watch, I realized it was already 1:00 PM. I sprinted back to the room Gerald had assigned to me, hoping Dr. Jeff would be a little late.

Relief spread through my body like a wildfire; Dr. Jeff wasn't there yet. I waited patiently for him, not daring to look at the files, for fear of him walking in at any moment.

"Hello there!" said a man who I assumed was Dr. Jeff. "I'm so glad I can finally meet you, Ms. Reyes! Every time you've been here before, a different doctor has treated you, lucky ducks."

"I've been here before?" I asked with a frown.

"You don't remember? Must be a side effect …" he murmured.

I was thoroughly confused at this point. I was a fairy? My parents were alive? And I had apparently visited this strange place multiple times?

"Turn that frown upside down!" he said. "It will all be over soon."

He took out the pocket watch I had tampered with earlier and swung it slowly back and forth.

"Think of all that is troubling you," he said in a monotone voice. "Imagine a whirlpool, slowly sucking your troubles away until nothing is left at all. Forget everything you have learned in the past forty-eight hours. You are Aimi Reyes, a normal human girl."

I could feel my brain slowly shutting down, but the urge to sleep was weak, almost as if the powers of the watch were not strong enough. That was it! When I had shortened the chain, the powers of hypnosis were weakened.

"When I count to three, you will emerge from the trance. One, two, three."

I pretended to wake up and tried to make my eyes appear glazed over.

"Good," Dr. Jeff said, still in his monotone voice. "Now, I want you to go back to the waiting room and forget this ever happened."

He began to walk away, but then faltered. "Oh, and don't try anything like you did on your little detour today again."

He gave me a flashy grin before shutting the door, leaving me shell-shocked.

How could he have known about me leaving this room earlier? Did they have hidden cameras? Or was it some sort of fairy magic? I guess I would never know. But if Dr. Jeff knew I had taken the files, wouldn't he have confiscated them from me? He must not have known.

Anyway, after Grandpa and I got back to the apartment, I immediately looked through the files.

My dad's file read:

Thomas Reyes

Gender: Male

Species: Fairy

Ailment/Reason Hospitalized: He was in the room when I told Andrea my plans. Also, I couldn't bear to leave her new husband alive and well without a proper punishment for stealing my dame!

Doctor Signature: *Dr. Jeff Tanning*

My file was the worst of all:

Aimi Reyes

Gender: Female

Species: Fairy

Ailment/Reason for Visit: Her grandpa wanted her to forget her heritage and live a "normal" human life. He thought that if she knew she was one of us, her energy would be too strong and the Patrol would be able to find her. The whole time he kept murmuring to himself, "It's all for her own good," over and over again. What a nutcase! She and her grandpa ran away before they could be deported; although, of course, they thought Thomas and Andrea had actually died. They thought that they must actually be the imposters. Aimi visits every few months, and it seems that a side effect of the repeated hypnotism has occurred. Whenever Aimi feels a strong emotion, she forgets what she did. I don't think this can ever be fixed.

Doctor Signature: *Dr. Jeff Tanning*

Once I read my file, all my memories came flooding back to me … my mom and I baking cookies; me walking Hammy, my pet pygmy dragon; and best of all, my grandpa and I getting along.

That file explained everything: why I didn't remember what I did to get sent to Miss Ranido's place and how I have blank moments sometimes.

Grandpa just walked in to ask what I wanted for dinner. He saw the papers spread across the bed and looked at me, his jaw slack, as if I had just betrayed him in the worst possible way.

"Aimi, what are those?" he asked, though his eyes said that he already knew.

I decided to tell him the truth.

I launched into a long-winded explanation of everything that had happened over the last few days. I even included the bit about Mr. Zoncles. When I finally finished, Grandpa stared at me, his face blank.

He said, "I see," and then left.

What was that supposed to mean? Was I in trouble? Was he going to send me to Miss Ranido's?

March 6, 2024

Once again, I woke up to the sound of Grandpa on the phone using his serious voice.

"… I didn't want to have to do this, but she knows now. It's not safe. The Patrol could arrive at any minute. I just want to keep her safe. So, you agree. She's a tough nut to crack."

Immediately, I thought of Gerald's response to my question about the *Permanent Residents* wing. He'd used those exact words. That could mean only one thing: Grandpa was going to send me to stay at Dr. Jeff's Emporium of Mysterious Maladies and Mishaps.

All the alarms inside me started to go off. I need to find someplace to hide.

I grabbed Mr. Zoncles and raced toward the window, onto the fire escape. As soon as I reached the landing, my watch started beeping and the hands started acting crazy. Then, once everything went silent, an audio recording started to play.

It was Dr. Jeff's voice that came out.

"You didn't think you'd get away that easy, did you? Didn't you think it was a little ironic that we had matching watches?"

The face of my watch popped off, revealing some sort of tracking device.

"See you soon, Aimi."

Then everything went dark.

Metaphor in Poetry

*In his poem "I Am From," Alex Rodriguez-Bader played with language, including the use of **metaphor** and imagery, with his mentor, Tasslyn Magnusson.*

Dear Reader,

What is a **metaphor**? It's kind of a way of using images to tell a story, and they are so important to poems. Alex's poem "I Am From" was filled with rich images and beautiful lines. I loved the line, "The darkness of my room that cradles me in its arms."

As we met for revision sessions, I learned a lot about Alex and the inspiration behind this poem. We talked about a lot of possibilities. We tried on different words and played with the space on the page to see if that helped enhance the meaning. So, just starting with one idea—metaphor and imagery—we touched on a lot of cool poetry things!

We discovered that Alex's poem had so many possibilities.

It was fun to test ideas out and explore language and poetry together. One of my favorite things to do is play with line breaks. Make lines shorter and longer. We did that. We worked on repetition of images to play with more metaphors. Alex tried everything!

It's a very important skill that all writers need. Willingness to play. And in the end, Alex learned one of the hardest skills of a poet. Alex knew what the poem was—and what it was not.

Not a lot changed about Alex's poem. And that's okay. Because through exploration and play and testing things out—Alex discovered the heart of the poem was there all along, and it needed just a little bit more repetition to tease it out.

Alex learned to hear his voice. And the voice of the poem. If you're writing poetry, you might try Alex's revision approach. Which was really to be open—and trust your poet gut. Think about cutting—maybe even try it. Know you can always put your lines back. You'll have fun, and you'll learn more about yourself and your poem.

Happy Writing!
Tasslyn Magnusson

As a fourth grader, Tasslyn Magnusson once tried to read her school library from A to Z, backward. She got stuck on P. L. Travers and Mary Poppins and has been reading anything and everything since. When she's not writing her poetry or working on her middle grade novels, she's reading fan fiction written by her teens and trading book recommendations with their friends. Tasslyn received her MFA in Writing for Children and Young Adults from Hamline University in January 2017. She has had several poems published and won the 2017 Room Magazine Poetry prize.

Alex Rodriguez-Bader

– Author Interview

Alex is in fourth grade and loves to use his imagination to draw and write. He likes creating fantasy—you can really use your mind to create things. He lives in San Diego, California, and has two moms, a brother, and the best dog in the world. If he wasn't writing, Alex would be having tennis practice and drawing and snuggling with his dog, Simba.

What changed when you revised?

Well, adding more things—repetition and adding more depth and details to my poem.

How would you describe a metaphor to someone who has never done poetry?

A metaphor is comparing two things—if there is crazy class it is a zoo or a voice that is beautiful is music. But you can't use the words *like* or *as*. Not using *like* or *as* really makes you think about how to compare things. It helps you be more creative.

Did you think you'd change a lot or a little?

Honestly, I didn't want to change that much, I was okay with tweaking, adding and taking some things out. But I didn't want to get rid of the heart of the poem.

Some stuff didn't change—how did you know the poem was done?

On the stuff that didn't change—it was things that I thought really described me and I couldn't let go of those lines.

What advice do you have for other Young Inklings who don't like revision very much?

If you are worried about revision, remember it's a way to make your story better—even by adding or taking out the smallest things—and won't change the meaning or heart of the poem, but make it better.

It was a learning experience—using your vision to learn about what you can do better in the future and helps you become a stronger writer.

What else do you have to share?

I was inspired to write this poem because it was a class assignment. I wrote it out and when my teacher told me about the Inklings contest, I thought this poem might have a good shot at winning. If I had to give credit about my win to someone other than me, I give credit to my teacher. She was really supporting me, and she helped me along the way; it wasn't a pressure to win. She said even getting rejected would be a huge compliment. I felt good even if I wasn't going to win.

I Am From

by Alex Rodriguez-Bader

I Am From

I am from the warmth radiating off my favorite giraffe,

I am from the sounds of the zoo, the birds screeching and chirping, making
their own music,

I am from the forests of Germany and Colombia always begging me to come
back—or is it me, begging to see them again?

I am from my parents' difficult family tree, whose vines are tangled through
many generations,

I am from my mom saying, "remember that!"

I am from the crabs that scuttle through the dark nooks and crannies of the
tide pools,
whose anemones have comforted me through my hard times.

I am from the ball spinning over the net,
Then bouncing off the hard concrete of my personality.

I am from Don't Stop Me Now,
whose soothing melody washes away my worries.

I am from Rachel and Kathy.

I am from a sizzling lasagna, and the hot chicken noodle soup whose smoke
writes my name.

I am from those nights when my mom snuggles me in my bed,
And the darkness of my room that cradles me in its arms.

Holding my favorite giraffe, I doze off until the next day . . .

Dialogue

Raya Ilieva worked with her mentor, Julia Hettiger, to revise her story, The Audition, *through the lens of **dialogue**.*

Dear Reader,

We spend our lives conversing with the people around us, but sometimes, it can be challenging to get dialogue right on the page. But dialogue is a good tool we can use to explore characters in our story.

In *The Audition*, Raya used dialogue as a tool to explore the relationship between her main character Sebastian and his brother Caleb. Through their words, facial expressions, gestures, and inner monologue—all aspects of good dialogue—we were able to learn a lot about these two boys and how their relationship shapes their lives.

I encouraged Raya to use this strength to further explore Sebastian's relationship with his mother. While the focus of the story is on the two brothers, Sebastian's mom also plays a significant role in his emotional state and motivations as a character.

In her revisions, Raya completed a series of

activities to prepare for the edits, including:

- **Freewriting snippets from the mom's point of view.** While these scenes didn't end up in the final story and the narrative remains in Sebastian's point of view, this activity allowed Raya to get an "insider's look" into the inner workings of Sebastian's mom as a character and more thoughtfully and accurately revise the scenes in which she's present.

- **Rewriting key scenes from the mom's point of view.** This helped Raya to ground the character in the moment, so when she was writing/revising from Sebastian's point of view, she was able to bring more details forward through the use of dialogue and nonverbal communication.

- **Rewriting the scene with an emphasis of slowing it down.** There's a key scene in the story where Sebastian is talking with his mom, and she's upset with him for walking in the rain and coming into the house soaking wet. This scene illustrates Sebastian's relationship with his mom, foreshadows what is to come, and gives the reader important context from past events. In slowing the scene down, Raya was able to show us more (rather than telling) through the strategic use of dialogue.

If you're writing a story that features a complicated relationship between two characters, playing with dialogue is a great way to bring forward this tension and emotion. I encourage you to explore writing scenes from alternate points of view, slowing down important moments, and freewriting to expand your own work. Even if this writing doesn't end up on the page, it can still help your story grow and flourish.

Happy Writing!
Julia Hettiger

Julia Hettiger is a writer from El Paso, Texas. By day she works in higher education, supporting the proposal development endeavors of academics, and by night she writes horror novels and books for kids and teens. She earned her Master of Fine Arts in Writing for Children and Young Adults from Hamline University in 2020.

Raya Ilieva

– Author Interview

Raya Ilieva is a fourteen-year-old writer living in the California Bay Area. She self-published a novella at age ten and a short story collection in her eighth grade year, and has also had her work recognized by several organizations. Her favorite things to read and write are realistic fiction and writing that blurs the line between poetry and prose. When she's not dancing competitively or playing the flute, she can be found listening to music, taking pictures of the sky, and wishing for rain.

What changed when you revised for dialogue?

It was the most I'd ever revised thinking solely about dialogue, and I was able to not only hone my skills but gain incredible insight into my characters. I hadn't realized that dialogue was such a powerful tool for doing that!

How did it feel to further explore Sebastian's relationship with his mom?

I had almost purposely avoided exploring their relationship because I knew very little about it, but once I started thinking about it further (through dialogue, mainly), I found that there were a lot of places my writing brain wanted to fill in, and the scenes I added made the story feel more fleshed-out as a whole.

How do you come up with your ideas?

I always write first drafts longhand in a notebook, and I never start a story with more than a sentence or two in mind. My ideas seem to come to me from nowhere, and then I have to keep writing to figure out what they're really about.

When did you start writing?

I've been writing for almost longer than I can remember—since kindergarten, when my teacher gave me a notebook and told me to try writing stories of my own. I'm so grateful to her because she guided me onto the writing journey that I am still on to this day.

The Audition

by Raya Ilieva

S itting at his desk, hunched in lamplight like a stock image of "boy studying," Sebastian's brother is unknowable. The lightbulb is a modern one designed to look ancient: the coil inside wiry and shining, the copper almost on fire. The way their window, just one of many in a grid on the apartment building, is positioned, Caleb is nearly a silhouette—a silhouette plus a little color, a little texture.

From across the street, Sebastian watches Caleb slam shut a book, swivel away from his desk, and reach wearily for a clarinet, perpetually on its stand. His fingers move in shadow: flurrying is the right word. It is strange to watch him play and not hear it. Sebastian becomes conscious of the rain on his shoulders and the crick in his neck from craning his head to gaze at the high-up window. The walk back from school has taken a little over an hour and it's already dark, being winter. He stretches his neck absently. He does not know why watching Caleb has made him so sad.

Inside, the sound becomes more and more discernible as Sebastian ascends floors. He's decided to take the stairs; he's not exactly sure why. It's fun at first, but by floor eleven not so much, and he enters the apartment breathing hard.

Caleb is still playing. Caleb is always playing.

Sebastian stays a bit in the doorway, watching the ceiling lights play with the shadows on his mother's face. She hasn't seen him yet; her hands grip a mug, and her eyes are to the dark, wet window.

He steps over the threshold. They both wince at the footfalls, and she turns her head. He walks into the dense silence and watches her face soften, then fall, then close up again as her eyes scan over him.

"Sebastian," she says slowly—she doesn't call him Bash anymore, not since the incident. "You're dripping."

"I am aware of that," he says carefully, and her eyes narrow as he slips off his shoes. "It is raining."

She rolls her eyes. "Sebast—you know what, I don't know why I even bother trying with you. Go take a shower."

Trying what? You've succeeded in humiliating me, great job, gold star, Sebastian thinks.

At the door of the bathroom, he pauses and looks at his mother: her thin shoulders, hunched, and the back of her head, small and unassuming. It is clear how tired she is and how much she has ceased to know him. Two strangers in the room who were once so deeply connected.

This is where I should feel pity, he thinks, and says, "Isn't it unfortunate that I have to walk home in the rain and the dark?"

"Yes," she says, unmoving. "It is unfortunate."

That's it, then, he thinks, and feels the impulse to hurt something with his bare hands.

Maddeningly, she takes a sip of tea. Bland liquid, hot for no reason, soothes and then strips your throat. He stalks past and disappears into the bathroom.

From the shower, Caleb's clarinet is potent. The mellow peals of sound; bright, jazzy notes. Sebastian looks on his brother's music stand more often than he would care to admit, to see the names of the pieces he's practicing. (He should be a little knowledgeable, he thinks, if he has to listen to them all day.) The Brahms quintet—he liked that one. Now it's that Gershwin that everyone plays, and the Nielsen concerto. Every evening Caleb does the *glissando* over and over again, perfecting who-even-knows-what. It's etched into Sebastian, too; he hears it in the silence when he wakes up. Here it goes again, right next to his head. The trill, long . . . and then up, squealing, to the resolution, which *is* glorious, he will admit.

Again. Again. Again. Sebastian shuts off the water forcefully, rakes aside the curtain, grabs a towel. He feels calmer but angry for not retaining his hissing fury. He slinks to his room, wondering how long Caleb will practice tonight.

At the table in the morning, Caleb eats cereal with such utter lifelessness that Sebastian wonders if he is an apparition or a ghost. His face is weighed down by its drooping tiredness.

Even without the fatigue, he and Sebastian are quite different. Caleb is all angles and lithe thinness, his musician's fingers bordering on gaunt. Brown hair, evenly razed in the back, falls over his forehead in the front. His lips are always the color of bruised cherries from the clarinet.

And Sebastian, Bash: "ruddy" is the word people use to describe his hair and complexion. Freckles. He looks jockish but does not play a sport.

"God," Caleb mutters almost imperceptibly, hand tapping lethargically on the table.

"I didn't sleep," Sebastian wants to tell his brother. Declare it, feel the meat of it as it hangs in the air. "It is the fifteenth night." But he doesn't.

Caleb looks old and worn down. Sometimes Sebastian disorients their ages—*Am I the older brother? Or is he older?*—before remembering that they're twins. It scares him how easily he forgets this most basic facet of his life.

Sometimes Sebastian feels so lonely he could choke and double over. Gripping your own hand tightly will never replace the absence of someone else's, and you can't hug yourself—you just can't.

The city they live in is not "aesthetic." It is not a curated mix of corners and buildings; sometimes the streets lead defiantly nowhere. Mailboxes hanging half open, a magnolia tree wilting in its concrete planter, and windows haphazardly open and closed bog the city down. The sunrises and sunsets are watery and clotted with the shapes of human settlement.

All this depresses Sebastian, makes him feel as though a rock has been placed on his chest. He finds himself yearning for uncorrupted views, smooth bowls of skies with trees that are crooked and flourishing. Air that is not muggy or hazy. Rivers. When was the last time he saw a river?

He can barely stand Caleb's clarinet anymore—he's tolerated it for so long, it's a miracle this didn't happen earlier—except for one night when he stops outside the apartment door and the piece is new and nearly topples him over in a bout of clear-headedness. But it's gone so quickly, the feeling seeping instantly from his mind. At school, teachers have started asking him, menacingly, what he wants to do with his life. They mention his perfectly average grades and lack of hobbies, implying a perfectly average personality. He knows this already, though. He lives with a prodigy who also works insanely hard.

The blogs he scrolls through at night reassure him that the world is falling apart anyway and the human species is deteriorating. They haven't met Caleb, he thinks at first, and then remembers who *he* is and agrees with them. He is just going through a fallow period in his life, self-help websites inform him kindly. He should not despair or give up. Talk to a trusted adult if you are experiencing warning signs. Stress and anxiety are often caused by lack of sleep, malnutrition, etc. Contact a trained professional if you experience severe apathy or boredom, extreme mood swings, violent urges, racing thoughts, panic attacks, consistent insomnia, lack of interest in food, loss of interest in activities you used to enjoy, feelings of hopelessness, paranoia, delusions, hallucinations, sleep paralysis, obsessive thoughts, compulsions to execute random behaviors, hearing "voices," altered perception of music or color, inability to hold conversations, or spiraling thoughts.

Insomnia is becoming a trend. CDC reports record a spike in suicidal teens, especially those who live in cities. Your semester grade has been released. You have five overdue assignments. Reminder: water the neighbors' plants. Sleep fools us into thinking that time has an order, when in reality, everything is a continuously unwinding string and it never—stops.

Sebastian, you could be so—

So much more—

Your brother works very hard.

All the resources available—

If you're struggling—

Don't hesitate to—

You must not forget what an important—

Priorities—

Could just be so much more.

Two weeks ago, Sebastian hurled a rock at his classmate. He barely remembers why he was so angry. Something was said, some snide or flippant remark made. He did not have a sense of impending dread that morning, as the questionnaire later asked him. In fact, it had been a comparatively normal day, until the comment. And they were outside, and the sun was so bright, it hurt his eyes, and the rocks were just right there: piled by his feet like a sign. And one had felt so nice and whole in his hands, so natural and pure. And suddenly his arm was very heavy, sore, as if he hadn't stretched it in a very long time, so the windup felt good. And once he'd wound up, he could not just drop his arm—he'd had to follow through. And it had sailed into the sun. And his classmate had crumpled beautifully, like art.

There were meetings, suspension, talks, this whole exhausting snowball of consequences. They seemed to think he was just such an unlikely candidate for violence. They made him take a survey, and then another. Crazy tests. He was too weary to lie. He wanted a reason. They did not expel him. His mother took away his license and made him walk to school, an hour each way. Otherwise, his life was unchanged: he still had zero friends and one twin brother. The violence dissolved into anger into sadness into indifference and back again. He stopped sleeping—that was the other consequence. He knows the world is waiting for him to repent but isn't sure how to.

Caleb was absolutely silent when Sebastian came home on that day. Their mother was fuming, muttering to herself, tossing objects aside. Caleb just smiled knowingly and retreated to his room. Another bout of anger flashed through Sebastian, hot. At school, his rage had been calm and controlled. But the apartment, usually a cocoon, was much too small.

He couldn't look at anyone. His mother became obsessive in her renovation projects. Throw pillows appeared and disappeared. A painting of blush-pink grapefruits in a white bowl was hung above the kitchen table; Sebastian liked the colors until he realized it was Photoshopped. He heard his mother briefing Caleb on the "incident" in hissy whispers, and Caleb laughed, bright and smooth, like his clarinet.

"He seemed to think it would be a good idea to …" his mother started this explanation, and Caleb said, "Oh boy."

"He threw something—a rock, I think the principal said—and gravely injured this poor boy, a classmate …" his mother continued.

"Just threw it? Just like that?" Caleb responded. Sebastian knew he was smiling in disbelief.

"Apparently. This other kid's in the hospital with a broken nose and everyone is so disturbed by Sebastian. Honestly, I don't know if he'll be allowed to return to school."

They continued on. In his room, Sebastian spun around in circles until he collapsed, nauseous, onto the floor, glad to feel something that wasn't anger or deadness.

Today, Caleb is pacing, rubbing his palms together, footfalls an incessant, tapping rhythm. He mutters to himself and is always playing an air clarinet. Sebastian finally asks him what is going on in the middle of the day, when the pacing is becoming much too much. In response, he gets an angry glower and a hissed, "My audition."

"What audition?"

"The most important one," Caleb says huffily and stalks away, which

Sebastian finds incredibly annoying.

"Maybe you can pace somewhere else," Sebastian retaliates, suddenly angry.

Caleb flicks his hair out of his eyes with a head toss. "No."

"I hate you," Sebastian mutters vehemently. He tosses a book to the floor.

The energy is tense, coiled, both boys wound tight and on edge. The clock leers at them. Hours pass in which Caleb practices furiously and Sebastian attempts schoolwork. It seems to them that blocks of darkness are hovering in the room, unmovable.

At 3:30 PM, Caleb's phone rings. He's at the sink, drinking a glass of water and, Sebastian thinks, practicing his mythical gaze. He picks up and talks to their mother. Then he hangs up and sends his phone skidding across the counter where it falls, neatly, into the sink. Sebastian laughs.

"Hey, idiot," Caleb says. "Mom's busy and you have to take me to my audition."

"Oh, sorry, I think my driving permissions were taken away? Indefinitely?" Sebastian says.

"She says they're temporarily back, just for today," Caleb says. "Come on, we need to leave."

"What if I don't want to?"

"I don't really ca—well, Mom said you have to, anyway."

Sebastian shrugs.

"I'm not ending my career because my stupid brother's too superior to drive me to an audition!"

It's a little fun to see him so distraught for once. Sebastian laughs at the word "career." Imagine having a career at seventeen.

"Bash. Please."

They stare at each other. The dark shapes in the air hum and pulse. Finally, Sebastian stands up. He is tired and doesn't want more consequences, capital C. He will never get his way because Caleb has a life and he doesn't. Slowly, he finds the keys and grabs a jacket. Caleb is already by the door, clarinet case in hand.

It is only when he's in the car, Caleb riding shotgun, that Sebastian realizes his confusion. "Caleb? Why can't you just drive yourself?"

"I don't have a license."

"What?"

"I don't have a license."

"Wait—but, you were studying for it—"

"I didn't finish. Not enough time."

Not enough time? Sebastian doesn't buy this. He frowns at his brother, pulling out of the driveway. The wheel feels good beneath his hands and his anger comes back. Caleb, thinking he's too good to get a measly little license, and so confident that someone will always be there to drive him wherever he needs to go.

The audition place is an hour away, which Caleb conveniently did not mention. They don't speak; Caleb closes his eyes. The "most important audition" is held in what appears to be an abandoned building, a school or an office. It is gray, concrete, and flat. Caleb gets out before Sebastian can decide whether or not to say good luck to him.

According to the car's clock, Caleb is out in an hour and a half, although to Sebastian, it feels more like five. It's 7:00 PM, and the sky has almost fully darkened, wind whipping across the even ground. Sebastian has been watching the door Caleb entered for almost the entire time, so he is jolted when his brother storms out of a different exit. He hasn't even bothered to put away his clarinet—he's clutching it in one hand, alongside the case—and his music flaps, loose, in the other.

The car door opens and a bitter gust of air slaps Sebastian in the face. In the dim light, Caleb's features are sketched only in angles and shadows; his eyes are murky hollows. He flicks the car light on aggressively and starts shuffling his music in his lap, organizing and arranging. His clarinet balances, quivering, on his knees.

"How did it . . . go?" Sebastian asks and immediately regrets it when Caleb turns to him and slumps backwards on the seat—eyes closed, his features falling wearily down his face. "Sorry," Sebastian chokes out, right as Caleb mutters, "Awful."

That's not possible, Sebastian thinks instantly, as platitudes and textbook reassurances leap into his mouth. He stops himself just before saying, *I'm sure it was fine.*

The whole duration of the audition, Sebastian was stewing in a kind of hatred for his brother; thick anger rose methodically into his chest as he stared at the horribly flat ground and equally bland sky. He was so tired of being angry—and he let it fuel him, better than food, water, air. Now, though, he is only tangled and empty: suddenly Caleb is crying beside him, the tears leaking out of his eyes in spite of themselves. He is silent, his eyes closed and his mouth twisted up into a tense bud.

Sebastian looks away. He feels as though Caleb has removed his heart and is holding it in his hand, gleaming and pulsing; it is too much. They share blood, and yet Sebastian doesn't know him at all. He feels a sharp, jolting pain in his chest, watching his brother slowly slacken.

Outside, the wind has brought in fog, and both are billowing in great clouds. The wind is almost visible, ribboning through the mist, sending it rolling and tumbling. Sebastian doesn't want to drive home—he can barely see as it is, and killing Caleb would not be a good look for him. He stares out the window and tries not to listen to the shrieks of the weather, or dwell on the fragility of the vehicle that ensconces him.

When Sebastian next looks over, Caleb has abruptly stopped crying. The tears: simply halted. He clenches his fingers together as if daring himself to give in. That—there—Sebastian realizes. Caleb is at war with himself. His hand limply clutches the ligature of his clarinet. Sebastian watches as he mouths words—*one, two, three*—and snaps open his eyes. He moves robotically, unscrewing the mouthpiece, removing the reed.

Sebastian stares at it, the ebony wood (Is it actually wood? He isn't sure), the mess of silver keys and holes that somehow Caleb knows how to navigate as seamlessly and mindlessly as tying his shoes. This object that causes him joy and, now, pain. He's built his life around it—filled with music what Sebastian has filled with anger, that void of twinness. And what if it fails? What if, stripped of his shell, Caleb and Sebastian are the same after all?

"You can drive," Caleb says quietly. "It's fine."

Sebastian shakes his head. "No, I don't—I don't trust myself. It's too dark. Foggy."

"Okay." Caleb's voice is barely audible.

"When do you find out the results?" Sebastian asks. He means to be friendly, but Caleb's features darken.

"Two months," he mutters. The unsaid words hover in the air: *two months of waiting, two months of agony, two months of not knowing.*

"Oh."

"Yeah."

I kind of resent you, Sebastian wants to say. Instead, he asks: "D'you ever ... I mean ..."

"What?"

"Do you ever hate it?"

"The clarinet, you mean."

"Yes."

Caleb sighs, clicking the silver keys, tracing the bell with a fingertip. "Yes. Yes, I do. Every single day."

"Oh."

"I mean—" Caleb shrugs and glances at the instrument in his hands like it's the most foreign thing he's ever seen.

"Then why do you torture yourself?" Sebastian asks.

Another sigh. "Because even if forty-nine percent of me hates it, fifty-one percent loves it," Caleb explains. "And it tips the balance."

Sebastian nods and does not ask if he has ever been fifty-fifty, perfectly torn, or if the balance has ever tipped the other way; he does not ask what Caleb will do if he doesn't make it past the audition. The car is still heavy, so heavy, with everything they have not said. But it doesn't threaten to crush him anymore.

Wordlessly, Caleb gestures to the window. Sebastian glances: the fog is lifting, ever so slowly. Methodical and even, it floats all at once.

"Odd," Sebastian mutters under his breath. Soon the night is dark and clear. He pulls out of the lot slowly and, holding his breath, merges onto the highway. Broken by words, the silence is fresh and new, swollen with potential, and he doesn't want to mess it up.

Caleb's grip on his clarinet is not so death-tight anymore. "Thanks for driving me," he murmurs.

"It's fine," Sebastian says. The road stretches on in front of them, eternal, unassuming. Inside a metal hunk, cruising over the pavement, the two brothers stare unflinchingly outward.

Character Arc

*Maya Mourshed worked with her mentor, Beth Spencewood, on a revision focused on Maya's character, Zero, and his **character arc** in Maya's story, Outnumbered.*

Dear Reader,

I was delighted to read Maya's mathematical world in *Outnumbered*. The main character, Zero, sees the inequities in his math-based world and decides to make things more equal, but of course it only makes things worse. It's fun to read about a character making mistakes and learning from them and gives them a character arc! While it's important that a character changes by the end of the story in order to have a **strong character arc**, it's also important that they are a part of making that change happen when it matters most. For this revision we focused on the one part of the story where Zero was missing in action—the climax. At the climax, Zero was incapacitated and only able to watch as the other numbers solved the mess he got them into.

We set a timer and Maya brainstormed as many

ways as she could think of for Zero to help solve the problem he got himself into before the timer went off. Once Maya finished, she chose the three ideas she liked best. We talked through how each would work in the story until Maya chose her favorite— the one you get to enjoy reading today!

Here are two questions to ask yourself if you're wondering if a story you are revising has a strong character arc.

1. Does your character make mistakes based on who they are at the beginning of the story? Characters need to try and fail in order to learn! If you realize your character is more of an observer than a do-er, brainstorm ways to have them act on what they believe and what kind of messes they can get into.

2. Does your character have an active role in their own change? If your character isn't around during that final climactic scene, or sits back letting someone else fix it for them, it will not be as satisfying to your reader. Readers want to see the characters act on the change they've had throughout the book and show what they learned in their actions.

If you want to brainstorm ideas to give your story a stronger character arc, I suggest setting a timer for 3-5 minutes and challenging yourself to write down every single idea that pops into your head without judgment. The goal is to write down as many ideas as you can, even the ones you know you'd never pick. The more you let your mind go wherever it wants, the more your brain learns it's okay to experiment with new ideas and the more ideas you have to choose from. Once your timer goes off, choose your top three ideas and then apply them to the story, or better yet, talk them out with a friend. Then choose the one you like best!

Happy Revising!
Beth Spencewood

Beth Spencewood grew up in Minneapolis where she spent the long winters reading anything with a twisty plot and writing science fiction stories starring her friends. She has an MFA in writing for children from Hamline University and writes middle-grade and young-adult novels. She works for Society of Young Inklings where she mentors youth authors and is the director of their youth publication programs. In her free time you can find her playing games of the board, card, or video game varieties, learning a new craft, swimming, or finding her way out of an escape room.

Maya Mourshed

– Author Interview

Maya Mourshed is in sixth grade and lives in Maryland. She likes science, math, art, poetry, and music. Maya plays the piano and is learning to speak Spanish. In her free time, she enjoys drawing, writing poems and short stories, and composing mashups, songs, and raps. She wants to be a chemist and musician when she grows up. Maya is planning to publish a short story and poem anthology called *Chemistories* with all her chemistry-related works, and is planning to put *Outnumbered* in another anthology titled *There's a Quadratic in My Attic!: Stories and Poems You Can Count On*.

What inspired this story?

Most of my works are inspired by my interests. Since I wrote a lot of stories about chemistry in the past, and I also made some stories about music prior to that, I thought, "What if I brought my math interest to life?" And so I began imagining a world of numbers, but then what could happen? Maybe there's some numbers that get noticed and numbers that don't get noticed. So I thought, why not have Notable and Neglected Numbers, but then who could be causing the problem? Maybe Zero is zapping the numbers with multiplication signs and turning them into zeros too, or something. So it eventually developed and I invented this city called Numbervana, which is located on a piece of graph paper.

You also illustrate your stories—what materials do you use and how do you choose what to illustrate?

Well, I kind of illustrate whatever comes to my mind. I have Crayola markers, Crayola Signature pens, and Prismacolor pencils. And the kind of pen that I use is Pentel EnerGel metal point pens. I usually start doing illustrations when I get excited about the concepts, and as the story flourishes, I start developing the illustrations even more as I take time to think it out. They basically come straight to me because I play everything as movies in my head. And almost as soon as I know the concept of the story, I can already make out an animated clip in my head.

What kinds of stories do you like to write the most?

Mainly stories that have to do with my interests and bringing them to life. You know how Pixar Animation Studios takes non-human things and they anthropomorphize them? I like to do that, too, with my stories. I consider myself as a one-person Pixar; I've also done that with chemical elements. I've done that with musical notes. I am now doing it with numbers.

What advice do you have for other writers who don't want to revise their story?

Well, I would probably say you could start by reading your story or poem aloud to yourself. And if you think that it needs a little tweaking, then don't be afraid to do that. Also, you could try to play your story or poem as a movie in your head. And if you think one of the scenes doesn't flow well or maybe the lighting's too dim or the sound effects are of not great quality, start there. That's basically what revising helps you to do.

What did you take away from this process of revising this story?

Well, sometimes when I come to a part of a story where the main character or a group of characters are in a big crisis, it's kind of hard for me to write those parts because I'm rarely in those types of experiences. The revision was mainly about making Zero more a part of the solution and less a part of the problem. I remember there was this quote on a poster at school that read, "You can only make a difference when you add yourself to the equation." It was actually kind of emotion-sparking for me because it made me feel a bit emotional inside when Zero started communicating something nonverbally. He made himself part of the equation in the revision.

Have you read any good books lately?

Well, there is a book that I read recently for history class. It's called *Red Scarf Girl: A Memoir of the Cultural Revolution* by Ji-Li Jiang about a girl named Ji-li Jiang who has a bright future in Communist China. But when Chairman Mao launched the Cultural Revolution, suddenly everything turned upside down because her family had a horrible political status. They worry about her future and when her father gets imprisoned; Ji-Li Jiang has to determine whether to be more responsible for the family or follow Chairman Mao instead. But my *favorite* book is *The Phantom Tollbooth* by Norton Juster. It reminds me of my favorite Pixar film, *Wall-E,* because I think they're both telling the same story.

Outnumbered

by Maya Mourshed

If you've ever seen a sheet of graph paper, you already know that it has a myriad of squares in an endless grid. But did you know that within those squares, on the coordinate plane, lies a city called Numbervana? It's the place where all numbers—from the well-known to the mainly forgotten—all reside.

Numbervana's landmarks include the expansive Multiplication Mall, where the numbers shop; Polynomial Park, where they enjoy the sweet aroma of operation-shaped flowers; and Fibonacci Fountain, which stands in the middle of the mall and has a nautilus-shell-shaped top that spurts water. In a large building called Cosine Cafeteria, the numbers dine on savory decimal points, fresh subtraction salad, and spicy tetrahedral tacos.

Today, in Cosine Cafeteria, the numbers gather as usual for lunch. There is a traditional hierarchy by which the numbers stand in line. At the front of the number line are the Notable Numbers—the popular ones who always get noticed. Everyone is envious of the Notable Numbers because they're rational, whole, and natural. The Notables think they're the luckiest and most perfect numbers in Numbervana. Stuck in the back behind them are the Neglected Numbers, who almost never get noticed. They are negative, irrational, and known to be quirky and just plain weird.

And then there's Zero, the most neglected number of all. He ranks even lower than the Neglected Numbers because he has no value. Zilch. Zip. Nada.

He sits all alone at a table, as usual. With no one to talk to, he looks around, watching the Notables and the Neglected. He sees the neglected Pi, Thirteen, and Negative Three. The three of them wait patiently in line to get their food, each holding a smooth tray with their stick-figure arms.

BANG! The cafeteria door slams open against the wall. Three Notable Numbers—One, Seven, and Ten—strut in with their stick-figure legs. Number One leads the way, his body shaped like a pole with a flag attached to its left side. Everyone stares and snaps photos as the three Notables flounce through the aisles toward the line.

Zero watches, wincing. One, Seven, and Ten push their way to the front of the cafeteria line. Pi, Thirteen, and Negative Three fall back.

"Hey! No fair! How come you always get to be first, One?" protests Pi.

"Because I'm the best, *that's* why," snaps One.

Thirteen speaks up. "And how come I always get stuck all alone in the back?"

"Because you're the unluckiest number ever made!" thunders Seven.

"So all we can do as Neglected Numbers is … be neglected?" asks Negative Three.

"Well," declares Ten, adjusting his snazzy, red-rimmed glasses. "The Notable Numbers are way more valuable than you are, see?"

Zero, whose eyes were fixed on the argument, identifies strongly with the Neglected Numbers. *Oh*, he thinks. *Those Notable Numbers are always so rude and arrogant!*

His heart sinks because he had often felt these same feelings of being inferior and dismissed by the Notable Numbers. When Zero was younger, he had wanted to try the parabola swings at Polynomial Park. But One and

Seven were playing on them and refused to give Zero a turn. They told him he was inferior to them because he was below them on the number line, and he was valueless. Even worse, he was "too round" to get on the swings. Zero could still hear them laughing as they mocked him. Humiliated, Zero had run and hidden under the exponential slide so that no one would see his tears. Even when he was raised to a positive exponent, he still remained Zero. Lonely, round, neglected Zero. Time and again, the Notable Numbers had excluded Zero from their activities.

Zero watches as One, Seven, and Ten get their food. The trio laugh as the Neglected Numbers are forced to wait. Then the trio passes right in front of Zero.

"Well, well, well," says One. "If it isn't zilch, zippo Zero."

"Yeah," adds Seven, "he's nothing but—*nothing.*"

"You heard him," echoes Ten. "You're a nobody, Zero."

Zero feels his brain heating up and his stomach getting queasy. He can see Pi, Thirteen, and Negative Three stare at him while cowering by the wall.

I bet they're worried the Notable Numbers will target them next with their mean words, thinks Zero. *If only I could teach those Notable Numbers a lesson! But how?* An idea suddenly strikes Zero. *What if I could make them feel what it's like to be a Neglected Number like me?*

He spies the multiplication signs on the kitchen counter that the chefs use to expand the food supply. Could Zero turn the Notable Numbers into zeroes by multiplying them by himself? After all, multiplying other numbers by zero equals zero.

"Those could turn the Notable Numbers into zeroes!" he says excitedly to himself.

While the other numbers are distracted, Zero sneaks over to the kitchen counter and grabs a bunch of multiplication signs. Then he hurls them along vectors at One, Seven, and Ten.

PEW! CLASH! POW!

"Yikes!" yells Seven.

The three Notable Numbers grab their trays and try to block Zero's onslaught of throws. But Zero is too quick. Seven rushes to the exit, followed by One and Ten. Caught up in the panic, all the numbers in the cafeteria get up from their chairs and rush toward the exit.

Zero follows, clutching the multiplication signs. Nothing can stop him now! Outside, he sees the Notable Numbers and the Neglected Numbers taking refuge behind Fibonacci Fountain.

A chaotic system unfolds, with unpredictability everywhere. For the first time in his life, Zero feels exhilaration and fear simultaneously. He'll show those Notables that they're vulnerable to becoming zeroes! And he'll show the Neglected Numbers he can go from zero to hero!

Zero climbs up to the cafeteria's roof so he can aim the multiplication signs with surgical accuracy. From high above, Zero sees that the Neglected Numbers are scared, trying to hide from his blows. But in the heat of the moment, Zero decides their fear is a price he's willing to pay to teach the Notable Numbers a lesson.

BLAM! ZING!

As Zero's multiplication signs hit their targets, the numbers immediately turn into zeroes and begin rolling in circles.

"What are we going to do?" yells One worriedly.

Ha! thinks Zero. *Now you know how it feels to be scared, like the Neglected Numbers.*

Seven shouts back, "If we can make an equation with Zero in the denominator, he will become undefined. Zero won't be able to throw the multiplication signs anymore!"

"But we'll need more than just us!" says Ten. "We need the Neglected Numbers, too. There's power in numbers, after all!"

Zero pauses for a moment. *Neglected and Notable Numbers working together? They've never joined forces and done that before!*

He watches the Notable and Neglected Numbers huddle together, plotting … something.

How could this be? They NEVER agree with each other! Zero realizes he's in trouble.

Terror overtakes Zero. He quickly hides behind the chimney of Cosine Cafeteria, worrying the Notable and Neglected Numbers are planning to attack him.

Number One shouts orders from below. "Ten! Thirteen! Time to make a division expression—you both go get a division line. Pi, you'll be up in the numerator. Me, Seven, and Negative Three will get Zero down and push him into the denominator."

Oh, no, thinks Zero. *They're going to undefine me!*

He watches in fear as the Notable and Neglected Numbers get into position. Then Ten and Thirteen return with a division line from Multiplication Mall. Pi jumps on top, in the place where the numerator should be.

I need to run! thinks Zero. *NOW!*

But he realizes he's out of breath. He's thrown so many multiplication signs and climbed to a rooftop! He is exhausted and can't run.

"Gotcha!" shouts Seven. Just then, Zero feels two sets of stick arms grab him from either side. Seven and Ten have him in their clutches.

"Stop! Get off me!" cries Zero.

Number One suddenly appears on the roof, laughing gleefully. "Didn't hear us come up the ladder, did you? I guess you were too busy throwing signs. Well, we've got you now!"

Ten and Thirteen work together on the final steps of the plan. Zero watches helplessly as the two push the horizontal division line so that it levitates above Zero's head. Zero tries to resist, but it's no use. One, Seven, and Negative Three keep shoving him downward, toward the denominator. Zero knows he's doomed.

"*Ohhhh!* What have I done?" wails Zero as he nears the denominator place.

He knows that as soon as he gets pushed under the division line, he'll become undefined. He'll be … valueless.

Zero is shocked that three of the numbers destroying him are Neglected Numbers. Aren't they supposed to be his own kind? But Negative Three is pushing him, and Thirteen is holding up the division line, which Pi stands upon. Zero has no way to escape.

CRASH!

"*Owwww,*" mumbles Zero. There, in the denominator at the bottom of the division line, he lies in a pile of shattered remains. He's too weak to say anything more.

But he can still hear. Zero listens sadly as the Notable and Neglected Numbers all cheer and high-five each other, celebrating their success.

"Wow!" says Thirteen. "I didn't realize how well and seamless working together would be!"

"Amazing!" says Pi. "We've officially become the first team of Neglected and Notable Numbers to ever collaborate. And we did it without a hitch! Our plan worked flawlessly and—"

Ten interrupts, saying words that come as a surprise to Zero. "I just realized something. We can't have a coordinate plane without Zero. Two perpendicular number lines need to intersect at Zero for Numbervana's coordinate plane to function! If Zero doesn't exist, then Numbervana won't, either!"

"But—but," blurts Negative Three. "We already shattered Zero. There's nothing left of him."

I'm still here, thinks Zero. But there's nothing he can do to bring himself back.

Maybe he could get the Neglected and Notable Numbers' attention? If he concentrates really hard, perhaps he can make his shards move?

Zero thinks about his plan and uses his mind to slam his white shards against the ground, causing it to quake beneath the numbers' feet.

"What's happening?" Pi shouts.

Suddenly, one shard, glowing with energy, slowly stands upright. It eventually starts scratching out something on the ground like a piece of chalk. Zero tries to muster all his energy and effort into providing a hint for the Notable and Neglected Numbers.

"I've never seen such a phenomenon before," Ten blurts out in shock. "How is that shard even *moving*?"

"Zero's—still alive?" asks Thirteen. "Is he writing for us?"

The shard comes to a rest on the pavement, leaving a message that reads: HORIZONTAL SLOPE.

After lots of deep pondering, One snaps his fingers. "I've got it!" he announces. "If we take Zero's remains and rearrange them into a horizontal line, then the slope would be Zero!"

Yes, thinks Zero. *That's what I meant! They understood my message!*

"But what if Zero starts throwing multiplication signs again?" asks Negative Three.

I won't! thinks Zero. *All I want is to be understood as the number I truly am, not as an inferior nobody.*

"I think Zero was upset with us Notable Numbers for calling him nothing," says Seven. "But the truth is we need him. And we should show it—just as soon as we bring him back to life."

Zero's mind is full of thoughts. *Everything has gone as wrong as it possibly could. My plan to teach the Notable Numbers a lesson was a total failure, and even my Neglected brothers and sisters fear me. Is there a way for me to make it up to all the numbers in Numbervana? What can I do?*

He valiantly tries to piece himself into a horizontal line so that he might be able to come back to life. But the broken shards of his body just can't hold.

Thirteen says softly, "I think Zero needs our help. Let's all work together again."

As Zero listens, all six Notable and Neglected Numbers walk toward his shattered body. One by one, they pick up his pieces, connecting them like a jigsaw puzzle on the coordinate plane until they form a straight horizontal line.

I am being reborn, thinks Zero. *I'm getting a do-over. I can **do** better and **be** better.*

Zero feels his broken fragments reassembling. They magically levitate and come together like interlocking crystal shards.

"Zero! You're back!" exclaims Pi.

Zero takes a ragged breath as he regains his balance. "Th-th-thank you," he says.

"Zero, before you say anything more, I want you to know something," says One. "We're sorry we called you nothing and were mean to you. Sorry to all the Neglected Numbers, actually."

Zero can't help but smile. "I forgive you. And I'm sorry I threw the multiplication signs and tried to turn all the numbers of Numbervana into zeroes."

"We know that you were trying to stand up for the Neglected Numbers," says Thirteen.

"Actually, we learned something important through this situation," adds Pi. "Neglected and Notable Numbers can work together in powerful and surprising ways."

"I agree," chimes in Negative Three, putting his arm around Zero.

"Turns out, Numbervana can't exist without you, Zero," says Ten. Zero stands as tall as he can. "The number line has a place for each of Numbervana's numbers."

The next day during lunch, Zero sits in the middle of Cosine Cafeteria, with the Notable and Neglected Numbers beside him. Neighboring tables also have Notable and Neglected Numbers sitting side by side. Zero is the happiest he has ever felt in his life, proud that he'd helped bring Numbervana's numbers together.

A thought strikes him: *What if they could stop thinking of themselves as Notable or Neglected? What if they're just numbers? Equal but different? Could they create a new mathematical property of equality?*

Zero smiles to himself. Then he says out loud, "Numbervana is the sum of all of us."

Word Choice

*Hollyn Alpert focused on **word choice** in her final revision of her poem, "Gold to Gray", with her mentor, Ann K. Morris.*

Dear Reader,

Poets like Hollyn Alpert love words. They love the sound of them, the look of them, and the ways they can be arranged to create beautiful imagery and lasting impressions. The words in Hollyn's poem "Gold to Gray" give substance to the pain of growing up that so many readers can relate to. Hollyn and I focused on word choice as we worked to revise her poem.

Hollyn's ease with figurative language turns the transition from childhood to the turbulent teens into something very beautiful. Childhood, she says, is "like cotton candy, sugar-coated strawberries that taste like heaven," whereas the teen years feel like "my fingers and palms were raw, scratched and bleeding scarlet ooze and desperation."

Hollyn alludes to another, very familiar, literary work to further characterize the end of childhood. "I was little red riding hood skipping on a cobblestone road, through a glittering meadow/sun-kissed hair floating like a soft cloud in the air," she writes of youth. But now, she writes, "i didn't know that instead of a kind old lady with soft silver hair/a ravenous gray wolf was waiting at the end of the road." Notice her use of capital and lowercase I's to differentiate between life stages.

Edgar Allen Poe once said, "I would define, in brief, the poetry of words as the rhythmical creation of beauty." Hollyn would certainly agree with this, as she herself said, "I like writing because it's like a space where I can put down thoughts and write them out and turn them into something beautiful."

Here is a revision method you might like to try, whether you're writing poetry or prose. Rewrite the following sentences to "turn them into something beautiful." The first one has been rewritten as an example.

The weather is bad.

Angry bolts of lightning staggered across a dark swath of threatening clouds, adding brilliance to the night sky.

Try it with:

I'm cold.

It's hot.

I'm worried.

I'm sad.

I'm hungry.

Happy Writing!

Ann K. Morris

Ann K. Morris is the author of the young adult novel *THIN*, published in 2022, and the middle grade novel *I Taught Benjamin Franklin How to Drive*, which will be published in summer 2024. Her first book, *Leawood: A Portrait in Time* (1998), is a history of a city in Kansas. Ann is a former middle school English teacher. She and her husband have two grown daughters and two grandchildren. They live in Colorado with their two dogs.

Hollyn Alpert

– Author Interview

Hollyn Alpert lives in California and attends a school for girls in grades six through twelve. She enjoys reading, writing, and art, especially pencil drawing. Some of her favorite books are young adult murder mysteries by Holly Jackson and *The Once and Future Witches* by Alix E. Harrow. Hollyn reads a lot of murder mysteries and plans to write one herself in the future. Her poem "Gold to Gray," which started out as a school assignment, won not only the 2024 Inklings Book Contest but also a Gold Key Award as part of the Scholastic Art & Writing Awards.

Where did you get the idea for your poem, "Gold to Gray"?

I wrote it because I felt like it reflected a lot of adolescents' journeys, and even some adults' journeys, as well. A lot of kids take their childhood for granted. They just want to grow up, put on makeup, put on a revealing outfit, and call that cool. But in reality, childhood is so special and golden.

What advice would you give to writers who don't especially enjoy revising?

I would say, *Don't revise it if you're not done with it*. You'll lose the idea of what the plot looks like. You want to write it out, no matter how bad it is, just write the entire thing. It's almost like a sculpture. First you sculpt the outside and then go in and fine-tune it with the details. You don't draw the eye before you shape the entire thing.

Where do you get your writing ideas?

Sometimes my ideas come from different things I read in books, and I just put them together and make a story. And other times I think, what if this were to happen instead of this? Let's say I'm at an assembly at school and something bad happens, and that starts a story. Or I take things that I'm interested in and I spin them into a story.

What's your favorite genre for writing?

I like to write fantasy fiction because I can experiment so much and not have anyone say, *Well, that's not realistic, or that's not real.*

What do you enjoy about writing?

I like writing because it's a space where I can put down thoughts and write them out and turn them into something beautiful.

Gold to Gray

by Hollyn Alpert

ages one two three four five six seven eight nine ten eleven twelve thirteen

golden years like cotton candy, sugar-coated strawberries that taste like
heaven

I remember when i spun around in pink tutus and unicorn leggings not
caring at all

i was little red riding hood skipping on a cobblestone road, through a
glittering meadow

sun-kissed hair floating like a soft cloud in the air, but now:

i don't spin. I stumble. I wear colorless, baggy cloth that I disappear in,
drowning in drab cotton

I remember feeling like having to balance activities academics sleep and
friends was hard

i thought it couldn't get worse—

i didn't know that instead of a kind old lady with soft silver hair

a ravenous gray wolf was waiting at the end of the road

I would give even my voice to return to one of those golden years

when i would sit with a group of friends and eat my lunch

when rumors about me seemed like the end of the world, especially from
those i trust...*ed*

at least i wasn't always alone

but now I'm alone, and nobody makes it out here alone.

and I'm being crushed by these mocking mountains of expectations and
   obligations
crumbling under the fragile weight of rabid responsibilities and ruthless
   reality
walking along the cliff, exhaustion snaking through every step
forcing myself to smile through it all, despite the approaching avalanche

those golden years are long gone
now a dim, faded gray

I remember when i was young, i longed to grow up
thinking adulthood was

opening sparkling champagne bottles of fizzy euphoria and colorful confetti

i thought being a kid was boring
little did i know how precious those slivers of heaven were,
thin glowing strings i didn't know i needed to cling onto until my fingers and
   palms were raw, scratched and bleeding scarlet ooze and desperation

now I know

and it's too late

Gold to Gray

Empowering the Main Character

Eleanor Yue revised her story, The Last Dragon, *with her mentor, Elizabeth Verdick. They focused on* **empowering the main character** *to shine as the hero of the story.*

Dear Reader,

Eleanor wrote *The Last Dragon* almost like a fairy tale, with a "Once upon a time" tone and a young character who hopes to right a past wrong. The heroine, Anna, is unlike all the other people in the town who fear dragons and believe they shouldn't exist. Anna longs for a day when dragons and humans can live in peace . . . and then she makes a magical discovery that sets her on this path.

When Eleanor was ready to revise, we talked about what *empowerment* means. How might she **empower** Anna in the story? *Empowerment* doesn't necessarily mean that the character is "powerful" or has magical "powers." An empowered character can be young and afraid. An empowered character can make mistakes. And an empowered character can find herself in unexpected trouble or danger, with no clue how to escape.

The important thing is that your reader gets to experience all of the character's foibles and frailties as part of the hero's journey. Readers want to root for a main character; they want to feel a sense of suspense and hope. Eleanor learned that she could focus more on Anna instead of letting the other character in the story—a dragon named Ember—take on the main role. After all, Ember was the *supporting* character, the one Anna herself needed to help. Without Anna, Ember was doomed to a lonely life on the mountain.

Eleanor originally had two perspectives in the story. She started the story with Ember, and then expanded into Anna's point of view until the end. Once Eleanor restarted the story from Anna's point of view and stayed within it, the character seemed more empowered—more of a "star." Next, Eleanor considered every event in the story and examined whether Anna or Ember was the one in charge. Eleanor found ways to make sure that *Anna* was the main one taking risks; Anna was the one making mistakes; Anna was the one to convince her people that dragons needed to be given a chance. In other words, Anna had to find the strength to help a magical creature and to convince her own father, the mayor, that the time for change had arrived.

That's empowerment: finding strength you didn't know you had. And that's our challenge as writers . . . to empower our characters to undergo challenges and give them room to change. Anna isn't the same girl by the end of the story. Her world is bigger, braver, and brighter.

Fly High!
Elizabeth Verdick

Elizabeth Verdick is an author of many picture books and nonfiction books for young children. Her picture books include *Peep Leap*, *Small Walt*, and *Bike & Trike*. She received her MFA in writing for children and young adults from Hamline University in St. Paul, Minnesota. Elizabeth has two adult children and three pets she adores.

Eleanor Yue

– Author Interview

Eleanor is nine years old and is in third grade. She enjoys acrobatics and learning how to swim. One activity she likes to do in her free time is to get a fuzzy blanket and a book and curl up on the couch. She loves any form of art, and big and small cats (the ones that live in the wild).

You seem like a fan of fantasy. What do you like most about reading and writing within this genre?

I think it's great how fantasy is a mix between real life and a magical world where anything can happen. I like the *Thea Stilton* books with magical creatures. It's fun reading about butterfly fairies and swamp goblins. Another book that I like is *The Girl Who Could Fly*. The children have magical powers but are forbidden to use them at their school. I like how there are unexpected turns in the story.

What did you learn in the revision process when it comes to empowering your main character?

I learned that you can make your main character stronger. In my story, the main character Anna went through some changes during revision. I had her take more risks, get into dangerous situations, and figure out ways to solve her own problems. Before revising, the dragon in the story wasn't the main character but was the one who mostly directed the story. To make my heroine more empowered, I had *her* direct the story.

Do you have advice for other young writers who want to explore magical settings?

Think of your characters first, and then think about the settings. Put them in settings that make sense for the character to be in, but let yourself imagine magical things. Fantasy books usually put dragons in caves or dens, so I wanted to do something like that. I decided on a mountain where the dragon could hide away from the town. I set my story in winter because I could imagine more natural disasters happening in winter.

Where do you get your ideas? Do you have a process for following through when a good idea comes to you?

I get my ideas from reading books, watching movies, traveling, and just living real life. My family traveled to Tahoe and that helped me imagine wintry settings. When I think of writing a story, I try to sit down and picture things in my mind first. Sometimes I draw the story events on a white board.

Are you working on other stories? Or other creative projects? Tell us about them!

I enjoy building stuff using everyday objects. For example, I'm making a dollhouse with four rooms by using objects that you normally just throw away.

You wrote about a magical creature—a dragon. But this dragon isn't scary; this dragon has a good heart. How did you decide to characterize your dragon in this way?

I like dragons a lot. I have read many stories where the dragon is presented as something dangerous and scary. But I wanted to believe dragons can be good, just like my character Anna did.

The Last Dragon

by Eleanor Yue

O nce, many centuries ago, there was a small village surrounded by a circle of mountains where a young girl named Anna lived. Anna was the daughter of the mayor and a curious girl who thought differently from the whole village. When most humans think of dragons, they assume they are monstrous beasts with menacing bodies and bloodthirsty jaws. But Anna loved dragons more than anything in the whole world.

One day a few years ago when she was eight, Anna was playing with her colorful rubber ball when she accidently made it go flying into the damp and dusky basement. She ran to the ball, desperate to catch it. But the ball crashed into an old mirror with golden swirls and angels on its borders.

BANG!

The mirror flew open, revealing a mysterious room. Anna spotted a dusty desk covered with folders. The folders contained papers with fascinating information about dragons.

Oh! thought Anna. After a few nights spent secretly reading the papers, Anna understood a hidden truth: *Dragons had once been united with humans!*

Knowing that, Anna tiptoed up the stairs and slipped into bed. She tossed and turned before drifting off to sleep. Each night after that, Anna crept out of her soft bed and into the creaky basement. If she told her father what she knew about dragons, he would be horrified. Anna decided to keep the secret to herself.

One night, Anna found information in the files about "the last dragon." A dragon that might be hiding somewhere near her village. All Anna wanted to do was to find this dragon. She decided she would go out looking for it some night.

A hard task, thought Anna. *Would it be worth it?*

Soon the perfect evening for adventure arrived. Anna's father had had a long argument with an unhappy villager and would be tired enough to fall asleep quickly. That snowy night, Anna grabbed her flashlight, quickly bundled into her warmest clothes, and tiptoed outside.

Minutes later, Anna stood below the towering mountain hovering over her town. Suddenly her flashlight shone on an amazing sight: deep, strangely shaped holes in the snow, with what looked like talons at the tip of each one.

"Footprints!" Anna gasped.

That was not all. Small sequin-like scales littered the ground. They looked hot enough to burn anything. Anna looked up, concerned. She could just make out more footprints zigzagging up the mountainside, all the way toward what looked like a mysterious cave.

A dragon cave? Anna wondered.

She hesitated, but the pull of curiosity drew her forward. She knew what she had to do—*climb*!

Barehanded, Anna gripped the rocks of the mountain, pulling herself higher and higher. Her hands were covered with snow, yet her palms got sweatier by the second as she climbed. Anna was persistent. Halfway to the cave, she took a break on a rocky ledge. Suddenly the rocks started to crumble.

This is the end of me! thought Anna. *Why did I choose to do this?*

Before Anna had a chance to move, the rock gave way and catapulted Anna toward the icy-hard ground. She closed her eyes, bracing herself for the fall. Just then, an invisible force yanked her upward. She landed on the chilly mountaintop.

Anna looked up to see who her savior was. A huge creature with glowing green eyes and fiery scales stared back at her.

"Oh no, the dragon!" shouted Anna.

That seemed to hurt the dragon's feelings because it lowered its head, sadly. Smoke drifted out of the dragon's nose. Anna did her best to calm her nerves. She gathered the courage to introduce herself.

"I'm Anna," she said, her voice shaking a little.

"Please don't be afraid," said the dragon in a kind voice. "I don't want to hurt you."

A dozen thoughts popped into Anna's mind, pushing her worries away.

Questions burst forth: "Are you alone? Are there more dragons here?" Anna asked. "How long have you been here? This is cool. What's your name?"

"Wow, you're the only human who's not scared of me," said the dragon. "I'm Ember."

"Is this your cave?" Anna asked.

The dragon nodded. Anna peered inside. On one wall were old rock carvings of humans and dragons fighting with sharp blades and balls of fire.

"What are those carvings supposed to mean?" she asked. "I've read a lot about dragons but never heard of this cave. Can you tell me more about this?"

Ember began to tell her tale. "A long time ago, humans and dragons were friends. Every day they would play together. Dragons warmed humans when winter came, and humans gave dragons homes and food. Humans cut down trees and built caves for the dragons near the village. Dragons built bonfires and cooked food while the humans hunted deer and small rodents. They split the meat so that each tribe could have an equal amount of food. That all changed one terrible day. The dragons were making a bonfire as usual when a young dragon accidentally created too much fire and lost control. The fired raged, and the dragons couldn't put it out fast enough. The humans were petrified. Finally, they were all able to put the fire out but there were ashes and ruins everywhere. The humans were furious. They banished all the dragons from then on."

"So that's why humans fear you?" asked Anna.

"Yes, and sadly I'm the last dragon here." Ember's eyes began to water.

Anna softly tapped Ember and said, "I'm sorry that happened. Can you show me where this all took place long ago?"

"I can show you what's left of it," said Ember. "You'll have to fly on my back."

This is really happening, thought Anna. *I'm going to ride a dragon!*

Ember lowered her back so Anna could hop on. As soon as Anna touched Ember's back, she felt a rush of heat. She examined Ember's scales and saw they were a mix of neon yellow, amber orange, and bright red.

The scales will keep me warm, Anna realized.

Ember flapped her wings twice and set off. Anna grasped Ember's back as, together, they swerved right and left. High in the sky, Anna saw glittering stars amid foggy clouds. The moon shone like an opal. Anna looked down at her beloved village. She saw dim lights peeking from the huts.

With two more swoops and swerves, Ember took a final dive and landed on the dry, hard soil of someplace unknown to Anna. She stared hard at the view. A whole village that had been destroyed was all that was left. She saw ashes as black as obsidian. Huge dragon bones spread across the soil.

"How long have those bones been there?" Anna asked in a low voice. "Did you know those dragons, Ember?"

"Those bones have been there for so long. They're all that remain of some of my friends," said Ember. "Maybe you've wondered why I'm the last dragon. When dragons were banished, I stayed behind, hoping that one day humans and dragons could be friends again. I knew I was sacrificing my family and friends. But I also knew my choice felt right."

Anna sighed. "I'd always wondered what happened to dragons in the past. And I've wanted dragons and humans to be friends again, too."

"Anna, as soon as I met you I felt like we shared a bond."

"Me too," said Anna. "Let's go back to the mountain. It's almost dawn, and the blizzard is getting worse."

They set off through the blinding snow. Ember flew hard while the wind howled fiercely.

"Look out!" called Ember. "Hail's coming!"

A strong gust of wind nearly blew Anna off Ember's back. She held on tight, as hail hammered down. Anna shielded her eyes and ducked her head, shivering.

"Here, this will help," said Ember. Immediately Ember's scales started to glow brighter. Heat burst from the scales, warming Anna.

"Thanks Ember," Anna said. "Oh, there's my village, below!"

Fresh snow and hail pounded on the huts, which looked about to tip over. The people huddled together in the heart of the village as, little by little, their huts fell apart in the storm.

Anna could see her dad. He was struggling to calm the panicking villagers. Many stood near the wood pile, trying to get a bonfire going. Wind blew fiercely, and the fire couldn't start.

Anna realized she had to do something to help. "Ember, can you bring me down to my village? I have to do something for my people. My dad can't do it alone."

Ember hesitated. But then she gave a slight nod.

As Anna rode into the village, chaos erupted. The people didn't seem to care how cold they were—they ran as fast and far as they could to get away from the dragon. Anna could hear the villagers screaming.

"Ember!" called Anna. "I have an idea. You can use your fiery breath to start the bonfire!"

Anna knew this was a risk. What if an out-of-control fire happened—just like in the past? What if Ember got hurt by humans? What if Anna herself angered the villagers and her dad? But Anna had no time to think everything through. She knew that Ember, with her help, could light the fire and keep the villagers warm in the blizzard. Anna could feel Ember draw a deep breath and release it. First, there was a gust of smoke. Then a glow of fire. And then the most amazing thing Anna had ever experienced began to happen. The bonfire lit up—and Ember stood back, looking proud but nervous.

Anna waved the villagers closer, calling, "Don't worry! The dragon just wants to help."

Slowly, the villagers left their hiding spots. They looked at Anna and the dragon in awe.

"Anna, what are you doing?" exclaimed her dad. "A dragon? Dragons are our enemy!"

Anna climbed off of Ember's back. "Dad, this dragon is named Ember. Tonight, she saved me from falling and from the storm."

Anna stood her ground, watching her dad's lip quiver. She hoped he wasn't disappointed in her. But Anna knew she had done the right thing.

She waited as her dad slowly stepped toward Ember, transfixed by her scales and glowing green eyes. He thanked the dragon, and then he smiled at Anna.

Turning, he made an announcement to the villagers: "Do not worry. Thanks to Anna, we are safe."

Anna smiled and hugged her dad. "I followed my curiosity and it led me here," she said. "I'm glad it did."

"Me too," said her dad.

The blizzard got milder as the days went on. Soon there was only a sprinkle of snow. Ember didn't seem to mind the snow, but Anna knew that Ember needed a safe place to stay nearby. So Anna, her dad, and Ember looked for such a place. They found a clearing with beautiful trees and a crystal-clear pond.

Ember's new home away from the mountain, thought Anna.

If you ever happen to pass by Anna's village, you might—if you're lucky—get to see the two friends happily playing a game they call "Capture the Dragon" by the lily pond.

Pacing

*Archer Xiang focused on **pacing** in his final revision of his story,* **Puffin Planet,** *with his mentor, Melissa Uchiyama.*

Dear Reader,

I believe that Archer Xiang's story, *Puffin Planet*, is a treasure. Archer quite naturally knew how to make a story with fast-paced excitement and moments that were slower in rhythm. What **pacing**! He provides sentences that are more general and also creates places that contain detail and multi-sensory description.

Archer knows that too much detail is ineffective and slows the story. Too vague and you cannot picture or feel a part of the story. Perhaps part of the fun of reading *Puffin Planet* is that these general sentences are also inventive and filled with imagination. The details, even the whimsical touches, can feel realistic because of Archer's solid writing. Like many of the great fantasy fiction stories, Archer uses what he knows of science and math as well as literature:

At first, Joey and Mark had a great time. There were moments of fun; sometimes they would turn the autopilot on, sit on the couch in the Astonishing Room, and watch their favorite internet personalities back on Earth. Their favorite episodes were when the people online tried to blow up expensive cars. For Mark and Joey, the episodes took their minds off the uncertainties of their mission.

Archer also pulls in details from his own life. The funny detail above about his characters watching such videos comes out of Archer's own encounter with a video. Archer also uses his own strong vocabulary to add strong imagery. Instead of merely narrating, he supplies us with evidence, clues, and scenes!

Archer could have written, "They were astonished" or "They looked around in awe," and left the narration at that. Instead, we see just what has gotten them into such a state of astonishment:

They looked around in awe. Rocky outcrops protruded from the side of a smooth cliff. Below the cliffs lay a huge and astonishing lake with hundreds of animals having fun. The grass reached as high as the trees. Beneath Mark's and Joey's feet, the ground felt as soft as a feather. The squishy surface of the planet was unlike anything they had ever experienced. The sweet air wafted around them like the swirling clouds in the sky. Apples larger than pumpkins swung on the trees, and ripe bananas were hanging from the edges of the leaves.

Using playful, descriptive language and thinking through the plot, Archer created a satisfying story that will be enjoyed again and again, in print.

Writers who also aspire to create memorable scenes like Archer may wish to scan or read aloud for places in their own work that feel a bit rushed or summarized, and then decide where they wish to go deeper and focus. It could be that you wish to add sensory details—lighting as many of the five senses, in smart ways, to engage your reader. It could also be that you add facts and information, sprinkling them in just the right places to create a world that is believable, even if it is a place of fantasy.

Like Archer, you can tie all of this together, not leaving readers confused but helping them to move through the story with enjoyment and clarity. You won't want it to end.

> *Mark did not want to leave his favorite old television, which was still stuck to the wall. Joey said that it was broken from the crash, so there was no point in taking it. Mark reluctantly agreed—and so it was. With Demesne on board, they would be able to keep contact with the Puffin Planet. Then it was time to show them how to work the new ship.*

What a thrill to read this particular story by this particular author. Every piece that you write can be a window into the way you see the world. Maybe it will be out of the small glass of a rocket ship bounding for greatness.

Happy Reading!
Melissa Uchiyama

Melissa Uchiyama is a writer and writing mentor

for international and Japanese writers in Tokyo, leading writing camps and workshops. She is an essayist, poet, and journalist, as well as podcast host, teacher, and champion of young people and their writing voice. She loves reading with her own children, too, and enjoys seeing what creativity buds from their minds. Melissa has loved her work with the Inklings Book Contest. She has also worked with magazines that publish young writers, such as *Under the Madness*. Melissa has been published in such places as *The Washington Post, LA Review of Books, Brevity Magazine, Kyoto Magazine, The Japan Times*, and more, with food columns and essays in anthologies. She is thrilled to see young writers find joy and confidence in how they express themselves in writing. Becoming published authors really seals the deal—they are writers!

Archer Xiang

– Author Interview

Archer Xiang is a kid who loves soccer. His wish is to become the best soccer player while also benefiting the world. He also likes gaming and programming. When he was young, Archer loved to play with cars. He also wants to be able to play many sports and obtain many jobs in his career.

Do you play music while you write, or does music distract you? What is your process?

Well, so I make the song very quiet and then I start writing. Like you can't really hear it, but you can get the rhythm of the song and it affects how you write the next scene.

Why are well-written stories needed in this day and age when we have TVs and internet personalities, funny videos, and sports? Why are good stories still important?

(Laughing) If you're a kid, like, parents won't let you play games for that long.

Why do you enjoy writing?

The reason I enjoy writing is because writing is a creative piece of work. Anything ideal can be added, and everything comes from your own mind.

How do you come up with your ideas?

Coming up with ideas can be like getting inspiration, or having things just spill out of your mind.

Who do you enjoy sharing your stories with?

I enjoy sharing my stories with family and friends because I can trust them to be able to understand my stories.

Puffin Planet

by Archer Xiang

Mark and Joey had been lifelong friends. After completing their training at the space academy, it was no surprise that they ended up in the space program together as shipmates. Joey loved rules. Mark, however, was adventurous. Because of this, Mark sometimes made a lot of mistakes. Although Joey was more disciplined, he never wanted to leave Mark behind. Besides, Mark was a lot of fun.

Nine o'clock in the evening of the fourth of January 2237 was their time for departure to Neptune. The spaceship was huge. At the front was the pilot's and co-pilot's chair. In the middle was an Astonishing Room with everything they wanted. Radios, cameras, and food were located in the rear of the ship. Energy blasted out of the turbines in the back.

The two astronauts had to be really careful of the dangers that awaited them. Monsters roamed the darkest parts of the universe. Huge asteroids flew at astonishing speeds. Unknown spaceships visited our solar system every year yet made no contact with humans.

Nine o'clock had come and the two astronauts climbed the state-of-the-art smashed-diamond ladder of the ship. Sparkles of light flashed around them as they entered the craft.

"On the count!" shouted the ground mission control commander.

Through his wireless microphone, the commander's voice filled the ship. Mark pressed the button.

Boom! They were off to Neptune.

At first, Joey and Mark had a great time. There were moments of fun; sometimes they would turn the autopilot on, sit on the couch in the Astonishing Room, and watch their favorite internet personalities back on Earth. Their favorite episodes were when the people online tried to blow up expensive cars. For Mark and Joey, the episodes took their minds off the uncertainties of their mission.

Over time, boredom had come, too. The days felt long and never-ending.

One day, something happened to change all those feelings. Joey and Mark were cruising along a few days after the blast off. The ship was straight and the flight smooth. Suddenly, lights flashed, the couch launched them at the TV, and images of the No Connection icon appeared everywhere.

A second later, Mark's and Joey's heads smashed on the top of the ship. They had lost connection with the mission ground control. The two astronauts had to go to the radio room, but it was too late. The force of gravity sent them shaking throughout the ship.

Boom! Things were falling over inside the ship.

"Mark, cover your head!" yelled Joey.

The ship spun around. Then something unexpected happened. The two astronauts were fired into a mushy grassland of trees. The ship had crash landed! After they checked for injuries, Mark and Joey suited up, packed some food, and left the craft.

They looked around in awe. Rocky outcrops protruded from the side of a smooth cliff. Below the cliffs lay a huge and astonishing lake with hundreds of animals having fun. The grass reached as high as the trees.

Beneath Mark's and Joey's feet, the ground felt as soft as a feather. The squishy surface of the planet was unlike anything they had ever experienced. The sweet air wafted around them like the swirling clouds in the sky. Apples larger than pumpkins swung on the trees, and ripe bananas were hanging from the edges of the leaves.

Sighing, Joey sat on a stump. He wondered why they had crashed. Mark seemed to be in better spirits. He thought he heard something close by and scanned the marshy ground. He spotted something that appeared behind a leafy bush. The figure noticed Mark and dashed away.

Mark quickly sprang into action and sprinted off towards the figure.

Joey shouted at Mark, "Hey! Wait!"

Joey sprang off the stump and chased after his friend, without really knowing what was going on.

The figure started slowing down, and Mark was catching up. Mark threw himself forward at the figure. After all, he was just chasing a little soldier puffin, so he wasn't afraid. The small bird headed toward a statue of a puffin, which looked out towards a path that led to a great big rock.

Joey caught up to Mark just as the sky went dark. Soldier puffins appeared from all directions led by a mini flying saucer. The craft was like nothing the two friends had ever seen before! There was a salt blaster on two sides and two jets on the back that seemed to blow out nothing to propel the aircraft. But the most awesome part was the bottom of the heavily armed ship, which had green light blowing out.

The Awesome Puffin Military Leader became visible from inside the saucer. He was armed with a helmet, a laser shotgun, and a butter knife. Mark and Joey were trapped. Suddenly, the Puffin Leader climbed down a ramp leading to the ground and pulled out a piece of fish. He held it out on his flipper and offered to share it with Mark and Joey. He ushered them onto the saucer. They climbed aboard.

Winding past the trees, Mark and Joey could see the big rock more clearly. As the small craft sped straight toward the rock, the boys covered their eyes waiting for the boom. When nothing exploded, Mark peeked through his fingers. Zooming through the air, Joey saw an entrance opening to a landing runway.

The saucer flew straight into a glorious city!

A group of stores were packed tightly together in the center of the rock. A giant sculpture of the Puffin God *Chiquita* was placed in the center. Multiple giant saucers zoomed through the air, silent like a bandit sneaking into a bank.

Once inside the Puffin City, Mark and Joey did not know where to look first. There were so many sights to see!

Groups of puffins roamed around, and none of them seemed to be interested in the newcomers. The doors of shops opened and closed, as the puffins seemed to be in a crazy hurry. Mark and Joey wondered why there was so much activity. It turned out it was the Awesome Puffin Military Leader's birthday!

When they first entered the Great Hall, Mark and Joey were amazed. They did not know where to focus their eyes … there was so much to see!

The china cups lined up next to the shining plates across the long granite table. The stone walls glittered in the bright room. The marble chandeliers swung above their heads, while the sound of the chattering puffins filled the room.

The Puffin race was made up of all shapes and sizes. Although all were small, they had many different looks and styles of dress. Because this was a special event, all the Puffins wore their very best. Usually, the Puffin children wore tie-dyed shirts with comfortable shorts, Mark and Joey were told. Tonight, however, most puffin children were in formal clothes due to this very important event!

The smell of fresh fish wafted across the room. Fish was the puffins' favorite food, but the sweets table looked so delicious! An enormous cake was centered on the long table and covered with candles. Vanilla cream smeared the top layer of the cake, which had a strawberry filling. There were many smaller desserts as well, such as Red Velvet Cake, Fruitcake, and Whoopie Pies with fluffy marshmallow filling. The fruit from the trees that the boys had noticed outside covered the length of the table.

Mark and Joey were enjoying themselves, but they worried about their ship. They had around eighteen hours to get to Neptune to complete their mission. They decided their only chance was to ask the Puffin Leader for help.

Joey approached the Puffin Leader and asked, "Sir, may you help us?"

The Puffin Leader answered in a language the boys did not understand.

Another puffin entered the Great Hall and said, "Do you speak English?"

Mark nodded but Joey, standing behind Mark, felt suspicious.

The puffin introduced himself in a very British accent. His name was Demesne, and he was an important soldier. Another puffin approached the Puffin Leader and told him about the crash in the Great Meadow. This was Mark and Joey's chance!

"Can you tell us where it is and why you puffins never made contact with humans?" the boys asked.

Demesne translated the question.

The Puffin Leader offered them a deal. He would give them a new, technologically advanced ship and answer their questions—in exchange for bringing the Puffin soldier along with them on their journey. That way, the Puffin Planet could receive transmissions and learn more detailed information about the outer edges of the universe. Soon they were heading out the door.

The Puffins set out with Mark and Joey to visit their crashed spacecraft. The Puffin Leader offered one of his flying saucers to take the group back to the wreck. Once there, Mark looked through the saucer, trying to persuade a reluctant Joey to use the Puffin ship. One word brightened Joey through his boring brain-fog as excitement filled him. The word "Glad."

Joey realized that they could go faster and further with a new ship. Then Joey started complaining about how they wouldn't know how to fly the ship without Demesne helping them.

Once the group arrived at the wreck, they gathered supplies from inside the ship. They began the long process of moving their belongings onto the new, advanced ship. The Puffins helped transfer as much equipment as they could.

Joey and Mark went through the kitchen area and found some items for the Puffins to try. Mark pulled out an unopened bag of cheddar cheese popcorn and offered it to the Puffins. He included an unwanted granola bar and some chocolate chip cookies. The Puffins were excited to try the new human treats. As the Awesome Puffin Leader chewed on the delicious snacks, he asked Mark and Joey if the Puffins could keep their ship from Earth for further investigation. He wanted to understand Earth's history and technology.

Mark did not want to leave his favorite old television, which was still stuck to the wall. Joey said that it was broken from the crash, so there was no point in taking it. Mark reluctantly agreed—and so it was. With Demesne on board, they would be able to keep contact with the Puffin Planet. Then it was time to show them how to work the new ship.

"C'mon fellas," Demesne said in his very British accent.

Three! Two! One! Blast off!

The spaceship burst into the night sky and disappeared.

There goes the saucer out of the rock with my new travelers, thought the Puffin Leader. *If only I could have gone, too.*

However, the Puffin Leader had too many responsibilities to leave on such a grand adventure. His people depended on him to take care of them. Mark, Joey, and their new shipmate Demesne were very much looking forward to their next adventure. There was still the problem of communicating with Mission Control. However, Mark and Joey decided that it was a problem for another day.

For now, it was time to head to the next planet with their new friend. The boys couldn't wait to see where they would end up next.

Motifs in Poetry

*Penelope S.S. Wong played with the use of **motifs** in her poem, "Growing Ambiguity," in a final revision of her poem with her mentor, Avalon Felice Lee.*

Dear Reader,

A **motif** is a symbol or image within a poem, which represents a theme or feeling within the story. To include a motif in your story, make sure it has a physical form—since a theme or feeling can be such an abstract idea, it is good practice to tie it down to something *physical* and *tangible* to ground the reader. For example, consider a plant—a physical object— which represents the narrator's emotions—an abstract idea. Now, great motifs evolve throughout a poem in tandem with a theme or feeling. Let's go back to our plant. How do we write the plant to evolve with the narrator's emotion? Here's an idea: Perhaps when the narrator is going through a low point, the plant wilts; when the narrator rediscovers joy, the plant springs back to life.

One theme that stuck out to me from Penelope's poignant poem "Growing Ambiguity" is, well, the theme of ambiguity—particularly, clarity morphing into ambiguity as the narrator grows up. The middle stanzas featured gorgeous images that convey this theme. When we met, we discussed the ways Penelope could refine this imagery so that it could better reflect the evolution of the theme.

One stanza originally described how the narrator finds gems which they later realize aren't real. Penelope then revised this stanza so that the narrator finds gems but realizes the gems might just be broken glass—after all, gems and broken glass can look quite similar. In this way, the evolution of this image is more aligned with the evolution of clarity to ambiguity—they share the same "internal logic."

Reader, if you're writing poetry (and even fiction!), you might evaluate whether your motifs share the same "internal logic" and are evolving in tandem with a theme or feeling. If not, consider how you can make small changes to redirect the images.

Happy Writing!
Avalon Felice Lee

Avalon Felice Lee is a writer. She received nominations for a Pushcart Prize and Best Small Fictions 2022. Her words are published or forthcoming in *Scapegoat Review, The Boiler, Brain Mill Press, Kissing Dynamite*, and elsewhere. She is studying creative writing at the College of Creative Studies in UC Santa Barbara. In her free time, she crochets flowery things and drinks matcha Einspänner lattes.

Penelope S.S. Wong

– Author Interview

Penelope S.S. Wong is in fifth grade. She enjoys writing poetry, short stories, and comics. In her free time, you'll find her reading, rock climbing, or doing math and 3-D puzzles. She also likes talking to people on airplanes, architecture, psychology, and engineering. In general, she gets excited about researching new and interesting things. Her favorite animals are octopuses, because they're smart, and Corgis, because they're cute.

What was the most difficult part of revision?

Receiving feedback can be hard because you work so hard on what you wrote, and it can be tough to see that someone wants to change some of it. But it's helpful to get other people's perspectives because things that might have been really clear to you might not be to someone else, since you've read your own work so many times. It helped knowing that edits are to improve the piece.

Why are metaphors important in your poetry?

In poetry (and in life in general), it can be hard to use words to describe certain things.

For example, try to describe what the color green is to a person who's never seen color. Or happiness to a robot. You'd probably compare it to something else so it's easier to understand. Metaphors turn things that are hard to explain into something that can be imagined.

What themes are in your poem?

Growing up and seeing that everything is not in black and white. I didn't start writing with a theme in mind, but as I was writing I started to see it. Actually, initially I had started writing a short story in verse from the perspective of a girl who had a father in prison, and at some point she realizes that his story is complicated. He wasn't either totally guilty or innocent. (At the time, I was reading a lot about prison reform and justice, and I got interested in writing about it.) But then as I started writing, I realized that this theme wasn't specific to the girl in my story. A lot of kids experience being confused about right and wrong and what's true in life while growing up. As I wrote, I thought the story would be better as a poem, and then it grew from there. Now it's less about this specific girl and her father's backstory. The poem is more universal now.

What question do you believe your poem poses to the reader?

Is it better to see the world how it really is, even if it makes life harder or more confusing?

Growing Ambiguity

by Penelope S.S. Wong

Before nine
nothing was blurry around the edges.

Before nine
no one ever lied.
At least that I knew of.

Before nine
all the questions had an answer.
And I didn't have to wonder.

I remember when
the color of your skin didn't matter.
But now I worry
I think it might.

I remember when
I would always find gems

as I dug through the soil,
and cry when Mom pulled the broken glass from my grasp
and stole all my pirates' treasure.

I remember when
I could always tell who the "Good Guys" were
and how I thought they always won.

I remember when
I thought the starting
line was the same for all.

I remember when
taller meant older
so it meant I could trust you.

I remember when
there was always an adult as an anchor
so that I could swim.
But I didn't know there was a time
I'd want to drift away.

Before nine
I never had to squint
but things looked clear.

And I remember when I turned eleven
I put on my first pair of glasses.

And although I could see further
color made things harder
to see.

Character Motivation

Rose Ferver, in their story, Hurry Home, *explored* **character motivation** *in a final revision with their mentor, Ashley Walker.*

Dear Reader,

Character motivation is the force driving your protagonist, providing the "why" that shapes your story. Why does your character want what they want? How do you communicate that through description, action, and other story elements? And when do you introduce these in your manuscript? Rose Ferver addressed those questions in a revision of *Hurry Home*, and you can learn from their answers.

Rose structured this story to keep the pivotal event (the one that altered the protagonist's life) a mystery until the very end. Their revision challenge involved carefully placing character-motivation clues to guide readers to the big reveal.

What are those clues?

Rose is great at creating descriptive details, and we leaned into this strength during revision. For example, in the opening line, the clouds are growing dark, hinting at the troubled thoughts of the main character, Jake. Across the story, natural elements like wind and rain echo his emotions. The weather also plays a practical role: it threatens to trap Jake at work on an important day. In the first scene, notice how his maze-like office building is physically and mentally difficult to escape. But Jake perseveres for someone special, and his journey ends in a setting that contrasts well with the office.

Beyond descriptive language, Rose brings character motivation to the page through the use of white space. They introduced short, swift paragraphs to show a sense of urgency in the office scene. By contrast, the longer paragraphs near the end slow the action, giving you time to build up imagery in your mind. That's where the clues come together, and Rose reveals the event at the heart of the story.

Developing character motivation can be challenging for a writer, but it's satisfying for readers. It ensures they understand the actions of your protagonist (and other characters) and invites them to care. I hope Rose's example will inspire you to work on character motivation in your own story.

Happy Writing!
Ashley Walker

Ashley Walker has been a primary school librarian, grad school lecturer, pilot, programmer, and personal trainer, but her favorite job is the one she's doing now—writing. Her broad life experience and education shape her work. Ashley holds degrees in Mechanical Engineering and Artificial Intelligence, and she recently earned an MFA in Writing for Children and Young Adults. She is the coauthor of the young adult biography collection, *Music Mavens: 15 Women of Note in the Industr*y (Chicago Review Press, 2022) and is currently writing a YA narrative nonfiction book about AI (Candlewick / MITeen Press, 2026). Ashley lives in the San Francisco Bay Area, where she's active in the kid-lit community and a dedicated mentor in youth science and art programs. Find her at ashleywalkerbooks.com.

Rose Ferver

– Author Interview

Rose Ferver is in seventh grade and lives in Philadelphia with their parents, brother, and grandmother. They like reading, writing, drawing, and frogs. They like writing mostly short stories and are currently working on a novel with their friends. They hope to write stories that move people and make them see how truly precious life is.

When did you start writing?

I started writing when I was eight or maybe a little bit younger. But I was only writing poetry because I was very inspired by Shel Silverstein poems that are really nice and funny and lighthearted (compared to a lot of other ones that are usually very dark and serious). I was young. I don't remember exactly when.

What's the best part of the writing process?

My favorite part of the writing process is probably those moments when you're really, really inspired. You've got all of these ideas and you're able to put them all out and there's just so much to add. And I really like that feeling of knowing exactly what you want to happen and being ready to just keep writing it.

How did *Hurry Home* change when you revised it for character motivation?

I tried to focus on the idea of how, in the society we live in, we're not really allowed to, like, stop and feel our feelings—not allowed to stop and grieve. You go through your childhood where you're allowed more freedom, but you're still expected to focus on school and very specific things. And then you reach adulthood, and you're pretty much just expected to work throughout your adulthood, in some way, until you physically are unable to. You just keep going until you either have enough money that you can stop young, or you physically are unable and you need help in some way. During my revision, I wanted to show that after all the character went through, after everything that happened, he is just now realizing this underlying lesson that was going on. He never got a chance to stop. And now that he finally has given himself a break, he actually has a moment to look at what was going on.

Do you have a favorite line in the story?

I don't think I really have a favorite line. But my favorite part that I, at least, thought was the funniest was when my main character was in the florist. He didn't know what any of the flowers were. It kind of helped add to his character that he never really bothered about knowing these flowers until now. And it also helped this idea that he's doing a lot for a particular person now.

What advice do you have for future Young Inklings who don't enjoy revision?

I don't like revision much either, but I think it can really end up helping your story. For example, I really hadn't thought about the amount of time that had gone by between a big event in my protagonist's life and when he came to terms with it. I'd just been thinking what's the math that's going to make this character a certain age and have some time pass by? Initially, I just kind of put down dates at random, because I thought it would be easiest that way. And I wasn't thinking about how much time had passed. It was actually very helpful to hear someone be like, Why is that? Because I really had not thought about that.

What are your writing plans going forward?

I'm working on a novel with one of my friends. She wants us to end up publishing that, and I don't know if we're going to, but we're going to at least try. And I'm also working on a short story, but I'm not really sure if I'm going to do anything with that one. I'm just kind of writing that one for fun.

Can you please share a few of your favorite books?

These are just books that I like: *The Giver, The One and Only Ivan, Deenie, I'll Give You the Sun,* and *A Psalm for the Wild-Built.* Those are some of them. I could go on listing them, but those are the ones that I usually think of.

Hurry Home

by Rose Ferver

The clouds were beginning to darken, and the wind was picking up. I glanced out the huge windows that covered most of the wall by my cubicle. It was 4:30, plenty late enough for me to leave. Normally, I would have waited out the rain and kept working. But I didn't have time today.

Turning off my computer, I packed everything into my bag and glanced down at my watch, hoping I would have enough time.

I left my cubicle, winding through the maze of miniature offices. My office was near the top of the building, with three of the four walls being huge floor-to-ceiling windows. The last wall was a set of elevators and two office doors that led to meeting rooms. Most people I passed were still working on some unfinished project they would always leave for the last second.

I hurried toward the elevator, feverishly pressing the down button. I tapped my foot in agitation, waiting for the elevator to reach me.

It finally arrived and I hopped in, immediately pressing the *L* for the lobby.

The elevator only made it down one floor when a huge group of people filed in, pressing every button between me and the ground floor.

Hoping the stairs would be faster, I ran out of the elevator and to the stairs. They were simple marble stairs, but they were as slippery as anything. I raced down as fast as I could, trying not to trip, and arrived at the lobby in a few minutes.

The lobby itself was a large room, with elevators at one end and front doors at the other.

The walls were white, and large gold chandeliers were dangling from the ceiling. The whole room was generic, and it did manage to look like the uninteresting office building it was. On one side of the room was the front desk, which was a simple bit of marble jutting up from the floor, and was the same color. The woman who sat behind the desk was named Martha. She was a stout lady, somewhere in her late forties or early fifties. She always wore a black dress, though the styles changed daily. Today she was wearing a simple sleeveless dress with a pearl necklace. Her black hair was pulled back into her everyday bun. Her face always looked a little overly painted, and today was no exception.

The elevator was still on its way down, so I took that as a win. I hurried past Martha at the front desk, not greeting her as I normally would.

"Well, Jake! Where are you off to in such a hurry?" she called after me.

"Sorry Martha! Can't talk!" I replied. I heard her chuckle to herself as I trotted through the glass double doors out onto the street.

The rain was pelting down, and I had to pause to put my umbrella up before I could continue. I marched toward my first stop of the evening. I pushed open the bakery door and breathed in the sweet scent of baking cakes. The room was long, with plenty of space for customers to wait in line, though there were none. The walls were a soft pink color, and simple cafe-style tables and chairs were set in rows along the walls. I went up to the counter and spoke to the girl standing there. She was a pretty girl, though a little unremarkable.

"Um . . . Hello. I'm here to pick up under . . . Lorraine," I said nervously.

"Of course! Your cake will be ready in a few minutes. Is that alright?" she asked.

"Well ..." I said, glancing down at my watch. "Yes, I can wait." I sat down at one of the small tables to wait.

After what seemed like ages, the girl called out, "Order for Lorraine?"

"Yes, yes, I'm here!" I said, standing up.

I moved to the counter and picked up the pale pink box that sat there. It was printed with the bakery's logo and had a small plastic window which I peered through, making sure it was all correct.

"It's prepaid for, right?" I asked, looking back at her.

She nodded and I almost ran out of the bakery. I put up my umbrella again and walked a few doors down to the small florist shop nestled between the dry cleaners and a Chinese restaurant. I pushed open the door and glanced around. The room was a small square, and the walls were lined with shelves of flowers from floor to ceiling, so much so that I could barely see the color of the walls. At the far end of the door was a counter, behind which a man was standing. His skin looked like an overripe orange. Matched with a muscular build and bleached-blond hair, he looked like a lifeguard somewhere in Florida.

I never knew what to get here. I inspected the different bouquets, pretending I knew what I was looking for. After going around for a few minutes, I pulled out my phone and called my older sister, attempting to balance the large cake in my arms at the same time.

"Jake? What's wrong?" the voice on the other end asked.

"I don't know what flowers to get."

"Of course."

"Which ones did you say she liked?"

"Daffodils and daisies."

"Right . . . right . . . which ones are those?"

She sighed and replied, "Ask the person at the counter. They'll know."

"Okay. Thanks. Bye."

"Bye, Jake. Don't be late."

I hung up and put my phone away. I walked up to the counter.

"Do you … have daisies … and … daffodils?" I asked, very unsure of what I was doing.

The man there nodded and produced a bouquet of mixed flowers. Not knowing what they were, I had to agree to them.

"That'll be twelve dollars and fifty cents," he said. "Is this for a girl?" he asked with a sly expression.

"What? Oh, no, these are for my niece. It's her birthday," I answered.

"Oh. Sorry. How old is she turning?" he asked.

"Nine," I answered quietly.

It struck me how long it had been. *How had I let the time slip away like this?*

He finished packing up the flowers and I paid. I left the shop in a hurry, knowing I was running late.

I jogged the last two blocks to my sister's house. I walked up the stairs of the stucco-fronted house and took a deep breath. I knocked once on the plain wooden door, then again, louder this time. My sister's husband opened the door.

"Hello, Mark," I greeted him.

He was tall, taller than me, and had dark spiky hair. He was very muscular, all of which was hidden beneath a plain blue shirt and faded blue jeans. His frame partially blocked the narrow hallway that led back to the rest of the house.

"Hi, Jake," he replied.

Out of nowhere, my sister pushed past her husband and hugged me. Her light brown hair attacked my face as her small frame—actually very similar in size to mine—pressed into me. I tried to keep the cake and flowers out of harm's way, but they ended up being a little squished. She was warm, and smelled like fresh bread, a nice distraction from the rain pelting down around me.

"Thank you, Jake. I know it's hard. But this means a lot." She pulled away and looked up to inspect me.

I surveyed her face. It was thin and long, just like my own. It used to hold so much cheer, always excited and happy, but after everything … it just looked like she had painted a smile on her face, trying to hide all of her pain and grief beneath it. It made me sad to see.

"Anything for Abagail," I replied, swallowing my emotion. My sister let go of me, and I handed her the cake.

"I guess … we'll put this inside until we get back." She handed the cake to Mark, who disappeared into the house.

When he came back, we all walked down the stairs and got into their car. It was old, and though it looked (and smelled) beaten up, it was still comfortable. I was soaked to the bone, but that wasn't important anymore.

"Alright," Mark said. "Let's go see our Abagail." He started the car and we were off.

We drove along in silence. We never said anything when we would go to see her. There wasn't ever anything to say.

After about fifteen minutes, we pulled to a stop. We slid into a parking space in the parking lot, which was almost always empty. Today was no exception. We got out and Lorraine took my hand and Mark's in hers. The rain had slowed and now was just a drizzle, but we were all cold and wet by this point, so there was no reason for an umbrella. We'd only be here for a little while anyway. I grabbed the flowers, and together the three of us walked up to the large brass gates. They were intricate, and I used to marvel at the complexity. But now the only thing I felt was a slight sorrow. There were so many memories here, some mine, but so many that belonged to someone else. We slowly pushed the gates open and stepped through. We walked along the path, and though it was paved, it was clear that it was hardly ever used. The path began to slowly slant upward, becoming an obvious hill. When we reached the top, we paused, surveying the land that unfolded before us. It was hills, like always, but rolling and far reaching. They were dotted with stones. A break from the bland buildings of the city.

We continued down the path for several minutes before we reached one part that wasn't a real path. It was just a patch of grass that had been walked on enough to be dirt. A large willow tree hung over it, and we had to push through the branches to continue on the path. It always made me feel like I was stepping through a portal, but it was never an exciting part of the story. We continued, slowly progressing to a slightly wooded area. We finally reached our destination. It was a single grave, set far apart from the others. The inscription read, *Abagail Reed, 2015-2019.*

I placed the flowers by her grave. And then I just stood there, looking down like I did every year. For the past five years. Lorraine cried silently, but we all just stood there. After what felt like years, the other two turned away and silently began to walk back the way we had come.

A thought occurred to me that I, for once, didn't squash.

"Hey, I'll meet you back at the car, okay? I just need a second," I called out to them.

Lorraine turned slightly to look at me. I wondered if she understood the battle raging inside of me, the one that had been for so long. But she only nodded and turned away. Beginning to walk back with her husband.

I swallowed and sat down on the wet grass by Abagail's grave. I tried to speak a few times, but my voice failed me.

"There are so many things I want to say," I finally managed to start. "Like, I wish I could see you grow up. It always breaks me a little more to think I can't."

"But then, I saw you grow up as much as I did, and I'm so grateful I had that time with you. You know, when I found out your mom was pregnant, I was so excited to be the cool uncle. The one that showed up to parties and gave you money even though your parents said not to. To babysit you and always give you too much sugar, just for me to give you back to your parents and watch them struggle with a sugar-high kid, knowing I got to experience all the fun parts."

I laughed a little to myself, the sad, quiet kind.

"And it happened a little, but real life got in the way. I had work, work, work. And when you went into the hospital, it felt like I'd lost my chance. I couldn't be fun and awesome with you. All the doctors said you'd be fine, and your parents were more than willing to be convinced, just in the hope you'd be fine and they could have the family they'd always wanted. But no. You were so young, you'd barely experienced the world, and then you had it all taken away—"

My voice cracked and I stopped. I put my face in my hands and tried to hold in what I'd blocked out for so long. I took a deep breath and started again. "Yeah. Yeah. I feel like I missed my only chance to experience a kid. I never thought I'd be more than an uncle, and I'm barely that. I'm sorry, kid. I never got to see who you'd become. And I'm sorry I waited so long to say this. It felt like you weren't really gone for so long. Or maybe I was still too stupid to think about anything other than work. But, I put off work today to come see you. So maybe I am learning. I hope that, if I can learn anything from you, it's not to waste my time. Maybe that's why I finally said something. I finally realized that no one has 'all the time in the world.' I'm

sorry, kid, I'm so, so, sorry. I feel like there is so much I'm still learning."
I laughed a little, but the sound of my own laugh made me sad. I cleared my throat and said, "Really, all I'm trying to say is, thanks. Thanks for being a kid. I miss you every day, even when I won't admit it . . . bye, kid."

The last part I said so quietly I could barely hear myself. I finally stood up and started walking away. I glanced back just for a second, and for that short second, I thought I saw the figure of a four-year-old girl looking at me. But then it was gone, and I was walking away, just as the wind slowed and the rain stopped.

Internal Logic

Kyle Chinchio revised his story, Long Time No See, *with his mentor, Betty Culley, focusing on the **internal logic** of the story.*

Dear Reader,

Kyle's revision for *Long Time No See* was focused on **internal logic**. What does that mean for a story?

Internal logic means that every plot or character element within the story grows logically and naturally out of what has been revealed before. For instance, if you describe the moon as being full one day, it's not going to be a sliver of a moon the next day, unless you're writing a fantasy story where moons change size like that. Or if your story or poem starts out with your character having a Golden Retriever dog, but then later on you say he has a Great Dane, it's confusing for the reader.

In other words, internal logic is a way of saying, *Does this make sense in the context of the story you're telling?* If it doesn't, it throws your reader out of the story, puzzling and wondering.

You might think if you're the one writing the story, you will catch any internal logic slips, but that's not always the case. Sometimes a writer gets so caught up in the plot or the setting or the dialogue or the description, that they miss seeing how the different parts relate to each other.

That's why professional writers have editors and copy editors and proofreaders look at their work, as all those extra eyes help ensure there is internal logic!

I won't go into the specifics of what Kyle worked on, because that would give spoilers for this terrific story, but I will say that Kyle was able to solve his internal logic issues in a way that made the story even stronger.

What are some ways you can check for internal logic in your own work? Being so close to your story can make it hard to see places where the internal logic is not working. Here are some ways to get a little distance or a new viewpoint.

1. If you wrote your story or poem on a computer or laptop, print it out and read it on paper. Or vice versa.
2. Try reading your story or poem out loud.
3. Share your work with a friend or family member. Getting feedback from another reader can be very helpful.

Happy Writing!
Betty Culley

Betty Culley writes young adult and middle-grade novels. Her young adult verse novels are *Three Things I Know Are True* and *The Name She Gave Me*. Her middle-grade novels are *Down To Earth* and *The Natural Genius of Ants*. She lives in Central Maine, where the rivers run through the small towns. She's wanted to be a writer ever since she was little and has really enjoyed being a mentor with the Society of Young Inklings.

Kyle Chinchio

– Author Interview

Fifth grader Kyle Chinchio lives in the Bay Area, California, with his mom, dad, brother, and sister. In his free time, Kyle loves to hike, read, play ping-pong, and of course, write. He sadly has no pets but continuously plans ant farms with his brother.

What inspired you to write *Long Time No See*?

I was inspired to write *Long Time No See* for many reasons. First, I brainstormed interesting ideas with my family. Second, when I write, I usually write about kids my age and put them in stressful situations.

What was the revision process for the story like? Was it harder or easier than you expected?

The revision process for the story was easier than I expected. For my story, we focused on internal logic and all I had to change was a few sentences. Even though I didn't alter much, it makes the story much stronger.

If you could only take three books to a desert island, which ones would you choose?

If I could only take three books to a desert island, I would choose a book about surviving on a desert island, *A Wizard of Earthsea*, and *A Wrinkle in Time*. The survival book would ensure my safety, *A Wizard of Earthsea* is action-packed and I wouldn't mind reading it again, and *A Wrinkle in Time* is a book I loved when I was younger.

Are you working on a new story?

Yes, I'm looking at a contest that focuses on the effects of climate change. I'm thinking of writing about experiencing a forest fire from an ant's perspective. An ant's viewpoint should be pretty interesting!

Long Time No See

by Kyle Chinchio

T he house reeked of must and neglect, as if it had been abandoned for several years. And, if it were up to me, it would have stayed empty.

"DANIEL!" hollered my dad.

Uh oh. My father never uses my full name unless I do something wrong.

He was calling me over to my room, telling me to stop dragging my feet (I had been watching a speck of dust get blown around in circles by the wind that crept in from the open windows) so I could finish unpacking my bags.

The four of us—my father, mother, fifteen-year-old brother, and I—just moved to Yellowknife Canada, perched in the northernmost corner of the country. When my father got a job offer that he couldn't pass up, we packed up our house in California within the week and left the next day. Back in my hometown, every day was sunny and bright, but here in Canada, gusts of wind blasted through the air, going right through my thin clothes and chilling me to the bone. The change was jarring.

The neighborhood I came from was tiny, and people rarely moved away. The last person I remember leaving was my best friend Paul Reza. I guess one of the reasons we were such good buddies was because we both were underdogs, each having only a handful of friends besides each other. We used to spend hours in the park until either his mom or dad called us in for supper. Whenever one of us got in trouble, you could expect similar things from the other. In other words, we were the best of pals, inseparable. None of my other friends ever matched him, and now I was losing them, too.

When I complained about leaving my friends, my brother Tim scoffed, saying, "Don't be such a wimp, Dan. Sometimes I forget you're eleven. It's not a big deal—you can make new friends."

Well, he wouldn't know. He makes friends so easily; it's as if he attracts them like moths to a bright light on an inky black night. He had already made a friend while we walked from our car, parked in the driveway, to our new house. In the few seconds I talked to the stranger, I found out that his name was Max and that he was around my brother's age. Max was walking his dog before he was intercepted by my brother. When the dog stopped by the road to pee in a bush, I looked at him more closely: the mix of black-and-white fur, with white dots running up his raised leg. I couldn't help but think the dog looked somehow … familiar. Soon, the dog finished and rushed after a squirrel. Max tugged on the dog's leash, and at the same time, was telling us that camping in this area was great. He told us that he loved the woods here and volunteered to take us exploring whenever we wanted.

But losing my friends wasn't the only reason I didn't want to leave my hometown. Our neighborhood was close-knit and had a number of unique traditions. One of my favorites was a massive party at the end of the school year, sort of like a potluck. Everyone would bring a morsel of food— usually a family specialty passed down through generations—to share. I especially enjoyed the roasted potatoes my third grade social studies teacher,

Mrs. Smith, made every year. And tomorrow was the last day of school! My eyes welled up with tears, thinking about all the fun I would miss out on.

I closed my eyes for a moment, recalling the mass of aromas mixing, creating a smell that reminded me of my grandmother's lasagna and the pain of the scalding cheese on my tongue—yet still couldn't stop eating. Most kids would spend the entire time at the party talking but I didn't. I focused on the food tingling on my tastebuds. Aside from this assortment of treats, when we finished eating, the principal would always set down a hefty arsenal of card and board games like UNO and Monopoly.

My father took one look at my face and decided that we'd go on a camping trip while we were waiting for the movers to come. Soon, we were heading to the nearest camping store, where we bought two tents, some flashlights, a bag of marshmallows, baked beans to make with toast, and a flare gun, which honestly, I thought was overkill.

The next day, we set out for the woods with my brother's new friend Max. Once we found a clearing, we started to set up our tents and, I hate to say it, but Max was extremely helpful. My parents didn't know how to set up the tents because someone else had always pitched in the few times we'd gone camping back in California.

We hiked through the forest and looked at wildlife for the rest of the day. I saw six deer (two males and four females) and a giant anthill with red ants pouring out of it like ropey streams of lava. Even with all this, I didn't enjoy the hike very much. The day was hot and humid, and thick swarms of mosquitoes blanketed us.

My mother and father, however, looked ecstatic—they'd always loved camping but couldn't do it often. That was the only reason I tried to look happy too because, inside, I still felt terrible. But in a moment, I'd see the beauty Canada could offer and my perspective would shift.

When we returned to our campsite from our hike, we opened the canned beans and my mother spread the unappetizing paste on some toast. She said we'd better eat quickly to have time for S'mores. It took me a long time to finish the toast, probably because I was taking micro-bites and spacing out, looking around me. It was beautiful—the setting sun cast long shadows in the clearing—but my heart wasn't in it. I snapped out of it, shaking my head to clear it, and quickly finished my toast.

Nothing about this was good, not even the scenery, I told myself repeatedly.

My father took out five S'mores and gave each of us one. By now it was almost pitch dark, so after we scarfed down the treats, we put the rest of the marshmallows away and started stargazing.

When the moon had fully risen, bright lights flashed in the sky: the northern lights. Everyone was spellbound by the sight, even Max, who had probably seen this a million times before. The sky looked like rivers of light snaked across it—bold streaks of green and purple, and dots of white. That's when I knew that even though Canada was different, I was going to be alright.

The next day Max called my brother, and in the short time I had to see the caller's name on my brother's phone, I noticed the words *Max Reza* flash across the screen. Holding the phone out of my brother's reach, I froze and my heart thumped against my chest. With my brother still grabbing for the phone, I wondered if Max could be the brother in boarding school that Paul had always told me about. I'd never seen Max before because he came home very rarely, only during holidays like Thanksgiving and Christmas, when I was celebrating with my own family. If Max was Paul's brother, it dawned on me that Paul might also be here!

To make a long story short, I rushed to Max's house, and sure enough, answering the door was none other than my childhood friend Paul, though he looked different than I remembered, wearing glasses and braces. I wondered if he also thought I looked different. Taking advantage of my distraction, my brother slipped away with his new friend, but Paul and I simply stood there, looking at each other, wondering if it was possible, afraid to move in case it was all a dream, and that shaking too violently would break the spell. But all at once, the world around me unfroze and we were rushing together in a huge embrace, one that betrayed the heartbreak, longing, surprise, and finally ecstasy we both felt in that moment.

Sensory Details

Kenzie Lam worked with her mentor, Elizabeth Verdick, on a revision focused on the sensory details of Kenzie's story, The Art of Flying.

Dear Reader,

When I started reading *The Art of Flying*, my heart leapt. I recognized a kindred bird lover and was captivated by the lyrical words on the page. At its heart, the story is about a girl who has lost a loved one, and a wild bird separated from its roost. Could these two characters connect—safely? Could each one, in a sense, find home?

Kenzie thought about the animal-human relationship and how best to present it in fiction. Although *The Art of Flying* has touches of magic at its beginning and end, it's a realistic story, one in which cranes do not speak in words or have complex thoughts. In realistic fiction, how can a writer create a nonhuman character that comes alive for readers? One way is to amplify **sensory details**. Kenzie gave voice to the crane by imagining how it would sound and interact with the main character, Maggie, from a safe distance. Kenzie

229

also played with the senses of sight and touch to make readers believe every moment of Maggie's encounters with the crane. This exploration strengthened the bond between the protagonist and the wild creature she tends.

Along the way, Kenzie discovered that going into greater depth about their relationship meant rethinking some of the other human characters in the story. In a novel, there's room for a wide cast of characters. Not in a short story, though. Kenzie thought about which of her characters could "leave the nest," so to speak. She omitted two of them, and the story grew tighter and more meaningful as a result.

That's the thing about revision: it's a journey. As you revise, examine each paragraph, each line—does it reach into your reader's heart? How might you amplify the senses and emotions? Push yourself a bit harder as a writer—and reviser—to see where your story might go.

Let your words take flight!
Elizabeth Verdick

P.S. Look at the writer's intentional use of headings in this piece, too.

Elizabeth Verdick is an author of many picture books and nonfiction books for young children. Her picture books include *Peep Leap, Small Walt,* and *Bike & Trike.* She received her MFA in writing for children and young adults from Hamline University in St. Paul, Minnesota. Elizabeth has two adult children and three pets she adores.

Kenzie Lam

– Author Interview

Kenzie is in sixth grade at Hillview Middle School in Menlo Park, California. She wants to become an author, artist, or scientist when she grows up. When Kenzie is not writing, you can find her reading, drawing, or birdwatching. Her favorite animal is a crow because they are one of the most intelligent creatures and give new meaning to the word "birdbrain."

What inspired you to write about sandhill cranes?

I wanted to write about a bird that's important to California, which is where I live. Sandhill cranes are an ancient species and roost in California every year. I love birds and birdwatching. I think it's magical to be able to fly.

How did you go about adding sensory details for readers? What advice do you have for writers who would like to try this technique themselves?

I tried to add details whenever the protagonist Maggie was near the crane to try and capture how it feels to be so close to a wild animal. My mentor helped me add *onomatopoeia* to describe the sounds the crane made in the story. I think if you're trying to do this, it's really helpful to think of situations you've been in that are similar to the character's situation. Even if they aren't so similar, you can take real details from your life and add them into your story. It's also helpful to get a good picture in your mind of what you're trying to describe.

What are some ways that you strengthened the bond between Maggie and the crane, as you went back and revised your story?

When Maggie interacted with the crane, I tried to give it a little bit of character. I further centered the story on Maggie and the crane, instead of on other things that didn't contribute as much to the story.

Can you talk about your choice to start and end your story from the point of view of the crane? That was a very interesting choice for a short story that is centered on a human protagonist—and it's magic. Why do you think it worked?

I did this to kind of tie the two characters together and give insight about a bit of the crane's life that both the readers and Maggie might not know about. I think this worked because it introduces the characters in the prologue, and then wraps everything up in the epilogue for a satisfying finish.

Was this the first time you've done a revision based on another reader's input? What are your thoughts about getting feedback and using it to expand your creative vision?

I entered the contest a couple years ago and had the opportunity to work with a mentor through the Fresh Ink program. I think it's really useful to have a mentor. They suggest and catch things that you would've never thought about, and they push you to become better as a writer.

The Art of Flying

by Kenzie Lam

prologue

The young crane's graceful neck bobs back and forth, his head turning, scanning the marsh for predators. His ears, hidden behind his golden eyes, hear the alarm call of an adult, warning of the coyote in the nearby brush. The bird's wide gray wings nervously spread open then closed before he breaks into a run. His long, dark gray legs flit in and out of the reeds, his thin feet sinking into the mud before pushing away.

The coyote is a barrier separating the crane from his roost. The bird calls to the others, the clear, shrill rattle settling on the marsh. A few of his own call back, the faraway sound blending into the morning conversations of the songbirds. The predator and prey are alone, with only the panic of the crane and the fierce glare of the coyote hovering over the shore. The crane runs, the undergrowth surrounding his habitat soon dissolving into woodland.

Two and a half miles away, in a cabin surrounded by the earthy smell of pine trees, a twelve-year-old girl awakes to an echoing call, a sorrowful cry.

Coo-o-o-o!

The girl steps outside, wandering into the wooded forest littered with leaves. Her dark hair blows in the breeze, her slightly suntanned arms brought to her chest in the cold of a California dawn.

Her breath catches at the beautiful sight before her, one her grandfather had described to her many times in the past. There, standing amid the trees, something very out of place: a Greater Sandhill Crane.

believe

The glowing outline of the sandhill crane shines in the rising sun. As the bird draws closer, I can see gray and dusty brown feathers, and dark, long legs. The crane is part of the winter roost in the California Delta. Pop would love to see this, if he were still alive.

Long before Pop—my grandpa—died, he told me all about the cranes. We would watch them every winter break. It's winter break now, but Pop isn't here to see the cranes with me. When I was smaller, I used to sit on his lap when we'd go down to the marsh. He'd get all muddy just so we could sit together on the shore. Then he'd tell me what he knew about the cranes— how they flew here every winter, that he used to watch them every morning.

He told me that they were a protected species, that they traced back to thousands, millions, of years ago. Pop said that when a crane glanced at you, looked in your eyes, magic happened. And that split second of magic could last forever. Of course, I always knew that the cranes weren't magical. Neither of us believed in the dragon-and-fairy kind of magic. But we both knew the magic of nature itself. A crane could seem so fragile while standing before you, its wistful eyes almost peering into your mind.

But what is a crane doing here, now, in the woods? It can't survive away from the roost.

I notice that the young crane is small and scraggly. A juvenile—it doesn't yet have the rust-stained feathers of an adult or the signature red on its head. I'm guessing it's male. I wish Pop were still here—he would know for sure. The crane seems lost, calling softly in the shadows. I hear his loud trill, again and again. Nothing, no one, responds. The bird is alone. He turns in a circle, and then walks away.

"Maggie!"

I startle, hearing Mama's voice.

"Breakfast is ready!" she calls from the kitchen.

I stick my head through the door. "Coming," I say back.

I turn to take one last look at the sandhill crane. But he's gone. Almost as if the crane were a work of fantasy, a product of my imagination. I just have to believe that he was there in the first place.

take the first jump

My favorite, homemade strawberry waffles and an egg, sunny-side-up.

"Thanks, Mama."

"Anything for you, kumquat." She has been calling me kumquat, a tiny type of citrus, ever since I was born as a premature baby. "You know I'm not good at baking, but this is my specialty."

I smile. "It sure is."

Usually, I take my time eating breakfast, but today, I'm impatient to find the crane again. I wolf down two waffles and wash my plate.

"So fast today? It's winter break. There's no hurry," says Mama. "Can you wake up your brother for me?" she adds as I near the stairs. "Tell Seb his breakfast is getting cold."

I head upstairs. Seb's room is across from mine, and had been empty while he was away at college. But he dropped out a couple months ago and came home. He didn't want to study science or go to school anymore. He wanted to follow his passion—art. I used to like art, too. Drawing. Sometimes Pop would bring his sketchbook out to the marsh and we would draw together. He'd had this old pencil, wooden and painted black. He'd given me one, but the new pencil didn't have the same worn paint and comforting feel.

Since his death, I've had a kind of artist's block. I can't bring myself to draw anything. Maybe Pop was the only one who was any good at drawing. Maybe the fact that I drew with him made me *feel* like an artist, even though I wasn't.

I tiptoe down the hallway and prepare to pounce on Seb in his bed, but when I reach his room, he's sitting at his desk, typing on his computer. He's not usually up this early.

"Hi," I say. "Can I come in?"

"Sure," Seb says, not looking up from his computer.

I peek over his shoulder and see a website for his small business. The website has an abstract feel, with an artsy background and a modern font.

"That looks great," I say.

"Thanks," Seb grunts. "I just need to add some finishing touches, and I can start selling!" I can hear the excitement in his voice. By selling, he means his drawings. Custom sketches and inks.

"Well, Mama says to go eat breakfast," I say after a while.

Seb clicks something on his computer. "I'll head down—"

But I'm hardly listening. I'm wondering if the crane is still out there. I hope that by now he has found his way home, but I'd like to see him again. I head to my room, slip a hoodie over my pajamas, and go straight to the little deck outside my window. From there, I have a perfect view of the woods.

flutter

He's there.

I spot the sandhill crane the moment I walk outside, at the corner of the fence surrounding our property. A heap of gray-brown feathers and rusty wire. *Oh no.* I look closer, realizing the crane is entangled in the barbed wire. I see bent and battered wires, the crane's wings waving helplessly. The crane must have entered through the patch of broken wire I'd known about but hadn't reminded Mama to fix. *Stupid!*

At a summer camp a few years ago, the camp leaders had said that if you find an injured animal in the wild, you must first assess the situation. That's what I have to do now: assess. I slowly creep forward. As I close the distance between the crane and me, he ruffles his wings, distressed and impatient. Scared. Worried. In pain. Things that I feel, too.

When I'm only a foot away—the closest I've been to a wild creature—the crane raises his head and looks up at me. His face suddenly seems almost human-like, with so much emotion beneath the surface. I'm so close, I can see details I've never noticed before—the golden streaks of each copper-tipped feather, the desperation in the bird's deep amber eyes. The crane makes a small noise, halfway between a croak and a chirp, almost as if pleading, please don't hurt me.

"Hey," I say softly. "You're going to be alright, okay?"

The crane coos at me, dipping his head. Like he trusts me. Or maybe has just given up.

Now that I've said those words aloud, though, I realize I don't know how to make them true. How can I keep the crane safe? I know I should tell someone about the injury, but helping the crane get free can't be that hard, right? Somehow, I want to keep the situation to myself. To help the crane all on my own. To prove that I can make a difference in someone's life, even if it's not a human life.

Everyone around me has their *thing*, but I don't. Seb has his small business and artistic ability; Mama has her cell discoveries; Pop had his bird-watching and the nature encyclopedia in his brain. He'd say, "It's all in here," and tap his head, and I'd always laugh, even when I was in a bad mood. He used to take me on hikes and point out every animal he saw.

But that was before. The doctors said that he'd been healthy, fit for his age, but that a heart attack could take anyone.

The last time I'd hiked with Pop was a year ago. Before he'd gone back to his apartment earlier that day, he'd said, *Leave the nest, Maggie. Spread your wings and fly.*

I hadn't thought about it much back then, but now I wonder what he meant. To come out of my shell, or to go on an adventure? To find freedom, or face a fear? Did it all mean the same thing? This moment now was just the start of my journey with the crane. The first flutter of feathers that might send me soaring into the clouds or falling to the ground.

The crane ruffles his wings again, yanking me into the present. I carefully maneuver the wire away from the bird's body, whispering *shhh, shhh*. I make sure to be careful around his sharp beak, but the crane doesn't try to defend himself. I almost want to pet him, comfort him. Even though he's a wild animal, I can feel his tangle of emotions as real to me as a human's.

As I move a wire away from the crane's wings, my hand brushes his feathers for a split second. They feel so soft, almost like fur. As my hand makes contact, the crane chirps, panicked. I part the feathers to find a couple of scratches from the wire. They're small, so I run back to the cabin to get a tube of antibiotic ointment. Outside the bathroom, I notice Seb giving me a strange, questioning look from the hallway, probably wondering why I'm running to the bathroom. I don't want him to know I have a secret. I hide the ointment in my hoodie pocket and walk out, trying to be nonchalant. Seb is already gone, though. That was close.

Outside, I look over my shoulder to make sure I'm alone. I carefully approach the crane, smearing the ointment on his cuts, hoping I'm doing the right thing. *Squawk!* The crane protests as I apply the medicine.

Finally free from the fence, the crane stands upright. At his full height, he's only about two feet shorter than me, his long neck making up a big part of his height. Someday, this crane will have a six-foot wingspan and grow to five feet tall. I expect him to flee from me now, but he stays, pacing the small yard. After a while, he settles, perhaps realizing I'm not a danger. I return to the steps of the wooden deck outside my bedroom so I can watch the crane pick seeds from the bushes. The crane seems calmer now, almost unbothered by my presence, so I stay.

I want the crane to be free, to find his roost and live among his own kind. But a selfish part of me wants him to hang around, to keep me company. A little secret for myself.

be careful

"Are you done with your application yet?" Mama is talking to Seb, as he picks at his spaghetti.

I'm trying to eat dinner quickly, but not so fast that they get suspicious. Seb has seemed a little wary of me lately. He'd found me outside a couple days ago and asked me what I was doing. He knew I didn't often use the deck. Thankfully, the crane had been standing near the side of the yard, where Seb couldn't see from his angle. Seb had wanted to ask me something then—I was sure of it. I could tell from the suspicion written across his face and the worried tone in his voice.

He's in his room all day, I convince myself now. *He can't possibly know about the crane.*

But all the times I'd noticed Seb lingering in the hallway outside my room made me wonder. I have to be careful the next time I see the crane— not just with the crane, but with Seb, too.

Here at the dinner table, though, I've been barely more than visible—while Seb and Ma spend dinner arguing about college. I take this time to think about the crane.

Pop had told me to *spread your wings and fly*.

I had already started this with the crane. I was in the air. All I had to do was trust my wings to lead me. To trust my own mind.

"Almost done with the application, okay, Ma?" says Seb. "I just need to, um, fill in a couple of things."

Should I help the crane go back to the marsh? I wonder.

"Well, finish it up today. Sebastian, the spring semester is coming soon, and you need to submit your materials by January."

Seb sighs. I know he doesn't like being called by his full name. "I know, Ma. But maybe—"

Maybe the crane could stay here with me, just for a little bit longer.

"No buts," says Mama. "You must go back to college. A good career is waiting for you."

I'll wait a few more days, I tell myself as I shove in another forkful of pasta. *Then I'll decide what to do with the crane.*

"Yeah, but my career doesn't have to be science—"

"*It should,*" Ma interrupts. "Art isn't going to make you much money. Get a good job first, then make art in your free time."

Just another week for the crane.

One more week can't hurt, can it?

prepare to soar

The crane hangs around for a couple more weeks. His cuts heal well, and I don't need to worry about them anymore. I check on the bird every few days, trying not to interact with him all the time. It's hard. Every day, I look outside when I wake up. When the crane's not there, I have to force myself not to go out and look for him. I care about him. What if the crane is attached to me—and what if I'm attached to him?

One morning, I see the crane pacing anxiously around the bushes. His scratches from the wire are now barely visible, and he's impatient to keep moving. The crane flutters around the clearing and walks in circles, but he has nowhere to go. I can tell he's yearning to fly, to escape from the limits of the trees covering the clearing. I need to bring him back to the marsh. The thought is painful, but a plan quickly starts to come together in my mind.

I know where the crane lives—and I'd walked the path many times with Pop, when the sunlight was breaking through the foliage like rays from individual shining suns. Pop would then tell me about times the cranes flew over the forest, hundreds of gray-brown bodies and flapping feathers. He'd said the sight was *mysteriously magical.* He used those words a lot. We'd go before noon, and sometimes we'd sit on a log to eat lunch. This time, I'd go in the middle of the night, take the crane to the marsh myself, and come back home. No one would know.

"Just one more night," I whisper to the crane. "Tomorrow you'll be back at the marsh with your family!"

The crane flaps closer to me and I smile. I can do this; my heart already feels like I'm soaring above the clouds. My plan is carefully mapped out—together, the crane and I, we'll take off.

But the crane will eventually fly away, and I'll stay standing on the ground, watching in the wake of wingbeats.

Later, I take a notebook from an organizer on my desk—the notebook that Pop had given me for my tenth birthday. I suddenly realize I haven't drawn in months. My hand lingers over the handle of the bottom drawer in my desk, but I force myself not to open it. Maybe another time. I'm not ready to face the things inside. Not yet.

Even though I don't draw anymore, I still imagine a beautiful sketch of a crane, the lines of pencil capturing every detail. I pick up a pencil and start sketching the crane, but when I try, I can't get the image anywhere near what exists in my imagination. I feel I'm letting down both the crane and Pop. I sigh and quickly close my notebook. The gust of air sends a small piece of paper fluttering out of the notebook pages. The poem "The Sandhills" by Linda Hogan that Pop gave me after I won Mrs. Keller's poetry contest in fourth grade.

That was two years ago, I think. *Back when I liked poetry, back when Pop was still around.*

I unfold the paper and read it. Its final lines make me glance back at the crane, standing on the leaves outside. The words bring me back to the marsh, sitting there on the shore with Pop and watching the cranes dance along to the swaying reeds. ". . . they stand, earth made only of crane/from bank to bank of the river/as far as you can see...."

That's where the crane should be, I think. *With the rest of his kind. Not here with me.*

The poem erases any worry I have about my plan. I read the entire poem over and over, letting the words sink in. I almost feel Pop sitting next to me, reading the poem over my shoulder. I can still see his warm smile, hear his deep laugh, feel his soft touch. In a way, the crane and I are similar. We have loved ones who are somewhere else. The crane probably misses his family the same way I do. But unlike the crane, I know I'm never going to see Pop again.

"Tomorrow night," I remind the crane, from my window. The bird continues to poke at the ground, innocent. He doesn't know what tomorrow will bring.

make the leap

"Hey, Maggie," a familiar voice says quietly, startling me at my desk. For a moment, I almost believe that it's Pop. But it's not his warm, low voice. I turn, dread settling in my stomach.

"Seb? What are you doing in here?" He looks as uncomfortable as I do.

"I . . ." He sighs. "I've seen you with that sandhill crane."

"How?" It's a dumb question, but suddenly I feel protective of the crane.

"Siblings know this stuff," Seb says. "And I know that you know my secret, too."

"That you're applying for classes in graphic design when you go back to college?"

"Yeah." Seb laughs ruefully. "There's no way I'm majoring in biology or environmental engineering, like everyone expects." His face gets serious. "Maggie, what's going on? It's not like you to keep secrets from your family."

I shrug and mutter, "I guess I just want something for myself."

"What about poetry? And drawing?"

"I stopped writing poems a long time ago. And you're the real artist in our family."

"Aw, don't say that. I know you've got some talent."

"But it's true," I say. *And you know it.* "That's why I need to do this—take the crane to the marsh."

"Fine," Seb sighs. "But I'm driving you. It's more than two miles there and back each way. It'd take you at least an hour to walk."

I feel slightly relieved. I *was* a little worried about going out alone. "Okay, but only on one condition. Please don't tell Mama."

Seb tears his hand through his hair, unsure he can make such a promise. Finally, he sighs and agrees. "Okay. Tomorrow night. We'll go after Mama is asleep." It seems to hurt him to say the words out loud.

It's true that we're hiding all this from Mama. I try to convince myself that it's not nearly as bad as lying—we're just not telling her the truth.

Those are two different things. Anyway, why is Seb so reluctant to hide this? It's not as if he never lies.

"Flashlight?" Seb asks. We're in the backyard outside my room, where the crane is sitting on the ground in the darkness.

I hand the flashlight to him, saying, "Check."

"Boots?"

"Check."

"Um, crane?"

"Of course." I gesture to the crane, now awake and looking at the beams of light.

I'd prepared a cardboard box and placed an old towel at the bottom for the crane to sit in. "Well, we've got to get the crane in the box," I say. I pick a few berries from the bushes the crane usually eats from, holding them in my outstretched hand. The crane tentatively walks toward me.

For these past weeks, I've tried not to make eye contact or form a bond with the crane, but have my efforts worked? If the crane has imprinted on me like I was his mother, he might never be able to live in the wild. I couldn't let that happen. I remind myself this is why I'm freeing him in the first place.

The crane's feet slowly cross the dried leaves as he moves forward. As he gets closer, I move my hand back toward me, leading him, until he is inches from my face.

"Soon you'll be back with your family," I say as the crane takes a berry from my hand. I try my best to gently lift the bird into my arms. The crane is lighter than I'd expected. He looks around, panicked, his feet scrambling under my arms.

"I'm sorry," I say softly as Seb helps me guide the crane to the box. I set the bird inside, his thin legs folded underneath his body. *We did it.* But we still have to free the crane at the marsh—the harder part of the plan.

Seb and I place the box carefully in the backseat of the car. I climb in beside it. "I guess we're ready," I say, clutching my left arm with my right hand like I always do when I'm nervous.

Seb starts the car. As we back out, he finally breaks his silence. "Don't ever do something like this again, Maggie, you hear me? Not just with the crane. With anything. You can trust Mama. You can trust *me.*"

"I won't hide stuff again. I promise."

"You sure?"

"Yeah," I say firmly. The one hundred percent, absolutely-definitely kind of sure. A tiny bit of regret seeps beneath my pumping adrenaline.

I shouldn't have pulled Seb into this. I should have just told Mama, and we would've brought the crane to the local wildlife sanctuary and everything would be fine.

The rest of the drive is silent, and I stare out the window at the dark trees, stars peeking above them, as I listen to the rough sound of the car tires across pebbly dirt. The moon looks as if it's painted, a glowing crescent shape bleeding onto a dark paper sky.

We soon arrive at the marsh shore, where the only movement seems to be the reeds blowing in the wind. But then, in the moonlight, I spot cranes dotting the shallow banks. Some sleep standing on one leg. I step out of the car with the box. At the path on the side of the road, I open the lid and let the crane step out. Together, we pick our way down the muddy shore, while Seb stays behind, leaning on the car.

When the crane realizes where he is, he coos softly. The crane is probably relieved to be home—maybe even happy. But the sound is like an eerie, mournful cry. I hug my arms closer to my chest. I should have brought a thicker sweater.

"Come on," I whisper. "Go find your family!"

The crane calls to his flock, the sound jarring in the quiet night. The trumpeting bellows of the flock fill the marsh with noise. *Squawk-rattle!* He turns around and his eyes face me, uncertain. And then I remember. *You're not supposed to let a wild animal form a bond with humans.* I hadn't been careful enough, had I? Now I've stopped the crane from living a proper life. I not only hurt the crane—but I've also pulled Seb into this when he's already dealing with enough, and I've hurt myself. I can't reverse the damage that I've done.

I think of Pop's words again. *Leave the nest.* I've left the nest, but all it feels like I'm doing is falling.

"Go!" I say sharply to the crane. "I'm sorry, but you have to go! Find your flock! Live your life! I don't care, just go!"

The crane skitters forward, and I instantly feel guilty for having scared him. Some of the cranes on the marsh startle awake and flap farther away, their calls echoing through the marsh and my mind. *Please, I'm sorry. I made everyone's life worse. I'm sorry. I'm sorry. I'm sorry.* But even a hundred apologies couldn't fix this.

My crane stands, frozen.

And then there are lights—bike lights—behind me, casting long shadows across the shore, sweeping a white sheet over the cranes' tense bodies.

"Magnolia!"

know when to land

Mama only uses my full name when she's worried or I'm in trouble. Or both.

"Ma!" I'm so exhausted, I don't feel anything but relief.

She stands in front of me as if she's shocked, even though she must've known enough to come here in the first place.

"Kumquat, what happened? Why?" The nickname comforts me, though my throat clams up at the question. I need time to prepare, to know exactly what to say. But the words spill out of me in ragged chunks.

"I . . . I found a crane, Ma . . . a sandhill crane. It was a little hurt, so it stayed outside my room, and I wanted it to be mine, my own thing, because you and Seb and—" I stop myself quickly, *Pop* almost slipping out of my mouth. "You all have your own *things* and I don't. I wanted the crane, and I wanted it to be okay. I wanted everything to be okay, but I was wrong. I can't do this."

I was so caught up in this *thing* with the crane that I hadn't realized I could've handled the problem safely. I'd felt like I was flying, soaring. I was so excited to be in the air that I didn't know when to stop.

"Oh, kumquat." Mama puts her hands on my shoulders, and then looks me up and down. "You're so tall now," she says suddenly. She sighs, or maybe just takes a deep breath. "I'm sorry, Maggie. I don't know how to fix this, but you can. I know you can do this. You can do whatever you set your mind to."

"Like what?"

Mama smiles. "Anything you want. I know you'll find your purpose in this world, kumquat. Very soon."

The words sound like something a teacher would say, but looking into Mama's eyes, I believe her. And after all the events with the crane, I finally have an idea of what my passion might be. *Wildlife. Birds.*

"Thanks, Ma."

"As I said—anything for you, kumquat. Thank you for telling me your side. Seb told me a little, but I didn't realize the crane meant so much to you."

"Seb told you?" First I feel confused, betrayed. Then I'm just glad that Mama knows and all this can be over soon.

"I had to, Maggie," Seb says. "I'm sorry."

"I'm sorry, too. For everything."

take flight

I'm sitting with Mama in the waiting room of the wildlife sanctuary, the crane nestled in a box at my shoes. The room has big pots of plants in the corners, standing out against the gray prison-like walls. But the air is hopeful.

I glance at the box, where the crane sticks his head out of the opening. *Squaawwk.* He fluffs his wings. I'm getting the sense he doesn't like being in cardboard boxes.

An employee walks around from the back and disappears through an elevator, and I realize—that could be *me* someday. I could volunteer here. *This* could be my thing, my purpose. Maybe I could help wild animals that need to be rescued. Like the crane. I look down at him, his golden eyes meeting mine.

A woman walks out to the front desk, and my stomach flips. "Hello," she says. "Welcome to the SPCA, what brings you here today?"

Mama looks at me. I know I should be the one explaining, but no words come to my mind.

"Um." I don't know how to explain my history with the crane. But I find the courage to tell the woman the truth. Or a version of the truth, I guess.

"I found a sandhill crane that was lost and it spent a couple weeks around me. I think it's a boy, but I'm not sure. He had a few small cuts from our barbed-wire fence, but I think they healed well. We figured it would be best to bring it here."

"You did the right thing," the woman says. She has us fill out a form about the crane's situation.

"What will happen to it?" I ask, nervous about the answer.

"It'll just spend a couple of weeks here, and then we'll release it back into its natural habitat."

The crane isn't doomed like I thought he was. The crane will be okay.

"Thanks!" I say, and then two employees take the box with the crane away.

Before the crane disappears behind closed doors, he looks back at me, briefly, as if to say, *Don't worry, I'll see you again.*

I smile. Maybe I will.

There's already an aching in my heart where the crane once was, rooted next to the space where Pop used to be. But I know I did the right thing.

When we get home, I quietly go to my room and unfold Pop's poem from my notebook, its worn folds fragile in my fingers. Just because Pop isn't here with me doesn't mean I can't be here with him. I open the lowest drawer of my desk, where our old sketchbook is lying on top of some of Pop's belongings. I gently pick up the sketchbook and go through its pages, flipping through all the time we spent together. Then I take the old black pencil from below, half the paint chipped off, and hold it in my hand.

The crane isn't outside my bedroom anymore, but I can still see him so vividly in my mind. His graceful neck, majestic wings, wistful eyes. I draw the crane, his expressive, insightful eyes, his delicate-yet-powerful wings. I draw him home at the marsh, surrounded by reeds and mud and other cranes,

> his black-tipped wings spread wide,
>> soaring,
>>> flying,
>>>> free.

epilogue

The sandhill crane, fully grown now, stands in the marsh, among his flock. He basks in the lingering light of the afternoon. By now, he has developed the distinctive red patch on top of his head, and his wings have grown a rusty brown. The crane calls to his mate, and she calls back as she probes the shore for food. The marsh is covered in cranes as far as the eye can see.

Above them, a blue airplane tears open the sky with a strip of white. Many of the cranes squawk, alarmed, but not the crane who once knew a human girl. He remembers how the human girl had brought him here that night a long while ago, how exhilarating yet saddening it was to see his family again. She had brought him home—and may yet return. The crane joins his mate, cooing gently, then raises his head and calls. The sound is powerful in the silent stillness of the mud and reeds.

More than ten thousand feet in the air, a girl stares out a plane window at the scenery below. She is getting closer to her California home. She smiles, recalling the events of her most recent winter vacation. Spending time with her brother, who had come home from art school this winter, and hanging out with friends from the SPCA. She'd never stopped missing her grandfather, but as her sadness crept away, the happy memories only got stronger.

Her dark hair is pulled into a bun, her hands pressed against the cold window. Her mind soars with every heartbeat, a steady flapping of feathers in sync with the fleet of wings below.

The Heart of the Story

*Henley Ferguson focused on the **heart of the story** in her revision of*
The Betrayal *with her mentor, Lisa Frenkel Riddiough.*

Dear Reader,

Children's book author, Anne Ursu, says, "The only thing a first draft has to do is exist." I love this so much. It gives me hope. Just finish the draft, and we will be on our way. However, what this also means is that the real work begins at revision. And sometimes we don't even know what the book is really about until we begin revising.

When I first read *The Betrayal*, I was immediately taken with the title. Talk about a hook! I couldn't wait to find out who was betrayed and why. After reading it, and learning the truth, I knew that our focus would be the **heart of the story**. What is it that you remember about a book when you've forgotten what the book is about?

When working with Henley on this topic, I asked

her first to tell me what she felt the heart of her story was. Naturally, she answered *betrayal*. And when I asked her how she wanted the reader to feel at the end of the story, she said, "I want the reader to feel betrayed, too."

With betrayal, there first has to be trust so that it can then be broken. Therefore, we looked at ways to demonstrate a solid trust between the betrayer and the betrayed. One of the ways that Henley chose to underscore the trust was to add a scene in flashback. I don't want to give anything away, so you're going to have to read the story to experience this for yourself.

Additionally, we took a look at word choice and figurative language as a way to reflect the heart of the story. Henley's story was already quite strong in this way. A reader might accidentally skim past her opening line, not realizing it holds a foreshadowing of what the protagonist is going to experience.

The train car rattled along the rails, jostling him from his peaceful slumber.

The protagonist's life is about to be rattled and jostled. The peaceful slumber of his existence is going to be overturned. A terrific first line!

In considering ways to bring out the heart of the story, ask yourself how you want your reader to feel when they have finished reading. What do you want readers to remember? Then look for ways to enhance those themes throughout your piece. It could be that you need an additional scene, like Henley chose to add. Or maybe a few key word choices will underscore the emotion you'd like your reader to feel. Either way, you might not know exactly what the heart of the story is until you begin revising.

Happy Writing!
Lisa Frenkel Riddiough

Lisa Frenkel Riddiough is a Northern California-based writer whose projects include picture books, middle-grade, and short fiction. She earned an MFA in Writing for Children and Young Adults from Hamline University. She is the author of *Elvis and the World as It Stands, Letters to Live By: An Alphabet Book with Intention, Pie-Rats!*, and the forthcoming picture books *Embarrassed Ferret* and *Furious Turtle* (Disney, 2025 and 2026). Lisa mentors youth writers through the Society of Young Inklings, is a former sales executive, an avid squirrel watcher, and a frequent baker of chocolate pound cake. Learn more about Lisa at www.lisariddiough.com and on IG @lisariddiough.

Henley Ferguson

– Author Interview

Henley Ferguson is a thirteen-year-old homeschooler from Olathe, Kansas. She lives with her family and her miniature dachshund, Fitz, and she loves all things creative. She is passionate about dance and loves participating in theater. She will never turn down a trip to a coffee shop or bookstore. Along with writing, Henley enjoys late nights, rain, bubble tea, and hanging out with her friends. Currently, her favorite book is *A Little Princess*. Henley has been writing for as long as she can remember, and she is thrilled for *The Betrayal* to be published in this year's Inklings Book.

Where did you get the idea for *The Betrayal*?
I first got the idea when I remembered a short scene I had written in a notebook a few years ago. I really liked it, so I developed the characters from there and the rest is history!

What changed in your story when you considered revising with a focus on the heart of the story?
The heart of this story, above all else, is betrayal. Trusting someone, and then later realizing that they weren't trustworthy after all. When revising, I decided to share another moment of true trust between some of my characters to make the betrayal all the more painful.

When revising, how do you determine which editorial suggestions to take and which to leave?

I always try to think about what I am trying to convey to the reader through the story. My mentor really helped me by having me try to see the true heart of my story, which is so important! When given advice and revision ideas in the world of writing, you should always remember only to change something if you feel it will make your story even better.

What do you most enjoy about writing?

One of the things I love most about writing is the fact that you can make anything happen. Nothing is impossible when it comes to fiction. You can, as the writer, travel to places you never imagined you would ever go! It is an escape from the reality of life.

What advice do you have for young writers who want to submit their work for publication?

Never give up! If you've gotten this far, stick with it. Have faith in your work and always remember that it is *your* story above all else. Never stop writing!

The Betrayal

by Henley Ferguson

Chapter 1

June 5, 1870

The train car rattled along the rails, jostling him from his peaceful slumber. He blinked and ran his hand through his tousled blond hair. How long had he been asleep? He turned his head to look out the window. The dark gray moors were barely visible beyond the thick fog covering the glass. He sighed and rested his head back against the wall of his compartment. He was alone … completely and utterly alone. The deafening silence surrounded him … enveloped him. His eyelids fluttered closed. He fell asleep again without another thought.

"Percy! Percy, come on!"

The dark-haired child pulled him by the hand, leading him down the hallway of the dimly lit house. Rosemary, his thoughts told him. The chandeliers above them jingled as they ran below; green pastures and unforgiving clouds flashed in the tall windows as they darted past.

The sunlight streamed into the car, forcing Percy out of his slumber. His eyes snapped open, widening with confusion. His dreams had always haunted him with strange meanings and patterns, but recently they had been different. They seemed to always involve his family. Were they trying to tell him something? Or were they just a force trying to distract him from what really mattered?

After their mother had died, it had just been the four of them: Percy, his older brother Charles, his younger sister Rosemary, and their father.

Percy checked his pocket watch; in a matter of hours, he would be home. His heart caught in his chest; he had to talk to Father.

Percy had gone over the conversation they would have in his mind for weeks. Would Father support his desire to pursue a career as an artist? Would he understand that Percy didn't feel the need to follow through with his societal expectations? Charles would understand, he always had.

"Sir? Excuse me, sir?"

Percy started upright. He had fallen asleep again. He looked up to find a train attendant staring at him expectantly.

"Can I interest you in a beverage, sir?"

Percy shook his head. "No, I'm fine. Thank you."

The man nodded in response. "Of course, sir."

But was he fine? Percy wished that he was at home and had already spoken with Father. There was no way to know how he would react. Percy looked around his car. The compartment was anything but lavishly decorated. The two benches opposite each other were wooden with flat red-velvet cushions. The walls were plain with a thin crack running from the top of the opposite bench to the ceiling. He once again turned his gaze out the window. Percy could see the sprawling outline of the city up ahead.

His breath quickened. They were in London; he was nearly home. He would have Father's answer soon enough.

Percy heard the raspy bellow of the train conductor announcing the stop. He hurried to collect his bags and exited the train. The station was bustling with passengers and travelers. The puffs of steam from the train's engine enveloped him as soon as he was outside. Soon, Percy was in a carriage bumping down the stone path that led to the heart of London. He had been overseas at an American university for four years. Percy had waited so long to come back home.

Chapter 2

Nine years prior …
London, England
1861

Rosemary suppressed a giggle, her icy blue eyes surveying the contents of the dark closet.

"Ready or not, here I come!" The familiar crow of his voice echoed down the long halls.

Rosemary giggled again, this time clamping her hand across her mouth, as to not give herself away.

"I'm going to find you, Rosey!" The faint sound of his boots clomped along the marble floors.

They got louder … and louder … until the footsteps came to a stop in front of the closet. Rosemary's eyes grew wide, and she slid down into the corner. The door handle slowly turned, and the door swung open with an eerie creak to reveal a boy of about ten years old. He had a regal posture, yet his grin was crooked and mischievous.

His light-colored hair was tousled in a playful manner, and his eyes gleamed a curious shade of gray. His eyes looked as though they belonged to one with wisdom beyond his years. Eyes from one who had seen much.

"Found you!" he cried, extending his arm toward her.

Rosemary grabbed his hand with a sigh. "Again."

"You know I've always got your back, Rosey. I'll always try to be there for you," he said, clutching her small hand in his.

She leaned her head on his shoulder, "I know, Percy. I know … you always watch out for me." She took a deep breath. "Now, let's go find Charles."

Chapter 3

London, England

June 6, 1870

Percy's eyes opened. These dreams … but this hadn't been a dream, it had been … a memory. The trees along the road cast shadows on the carriage; the brisk wind rattled the glass windows.

"We've arrived at Lancaster Manor, sir!" He heard the coachman call from up above.

Percy looked, yes, he knew this path by heart. He was home.

The carriage stopped in front of the manor, and Percy gazed at it, smiling. It was a very large white house; ivy vines trailed across the walls and windows. The six white columns stood tall as if guarding the door, but not in a menacing kind of way. The sky was a bluish-gray, and in the distance he heard a melancholy bird's song. Percy stepped out, ready to see his family again. His baggage fell into a disorderly heap near his feet, and he was just reaching down to collect it when he heard footsteps racing toward him. Percy turned around. It was Rosemary. She was sixteen now, her dark wavy hair flowing out behind her. Charles stood at the door. Percy's lips broke into a crooked grin as he held his arms open wide.

"Rosey, you've gotten so tall!"

Rosemary flung her arms around him. She was sobbing.

"He's dead?! He—he can't be dead!" Percy was sitting in the middle of the rose-colored loveseat in the parlor. "He was in the finest of health when I left. I—I—"

Charles looked like he hadn't slept in weeks. His dark eyes, usually so bright and high spirited, were shadowed with grief. His dark hair seemed disheveled and unkempt. When he spoke, his voice sounded gravelly and raw.

"Percy, Father … Father seemed at his best. He was the healthiest man I knew. We thought about writing you … but you would have already left by the time the telegram arrived."

"Don't!" Percy yelled at him. "Don't speak of him that way, don't say *was* and *knew* as if he hadn't been in this very room just days ago talking and laughing the way you know he did. Don't describe him as if he was nothing but a shadow of what used to be."

"Percy, I'm trying my best, all right?" Charles clenched his hands. They were silent.

Percy sighed. "… I'm sorry, I—I'm just not used to talking about him in such a way. You have known about it longer than I have. Did he leave a will?"

Charles hesitated before thrusting some papers into Percy's hands. Percy looked through it quickly and swallowed back a gasp. Everything was left to Charles. The house, the furniture, and the family fortune. All left to Charles.

Percy turned around, "I don't understa—" But Charles wasn't there. Percy didn't know what to say. There had to be a mistake! His father was the most generous man he knew, yet not a thing was left to his younger children. At that moment, Rosemary entered the room. Her face was tear stained, and her eyes were red and puffy from crying.

"Percy, I'm so glad you're home. Nothing was the same without you."

He looked at her tenderly.

"Did you … did you see the will?" she asked.

Percy nodded.

"We didn't even think he had written one until Charles found it in the back of the library desk drawer."

She sat down next to her brother. "I know it sounds naive, but I felt as though Father would never die, that he would always be here for all of us. It must be so different for you, to lose two parents … I never even knew Mother."

She started crying again.

"I know, Rosey. I know."

Chapter 4

Eight years prior ...

London, England

1862

ercy held his pencil in his hand, its dark strokes radiating down upon the paper. He tilted his head, it still needed something . . .

"Percy!"

He looked up to see Charles, his brother, standing over him. "So this is where you've been!"

He sat down next to him on the steps. The cool breeze whipped around their faces, the leaves rustling in the nearby trees. They sat in silence for a few minutes, staring at the painted sky. The sun gradually lowered into the tree line. Charles looked down at the papers his brother clutched in his grasp.

"Percy . . . that's . . . that's really good."

Percy looked into his brother's sincere face. "You really think so?"

"Of course, I do! Do you ever think about becoming an artist?"

Percy's eyes widened. "You really think I could be one?"

Charles hit his shoulder playfully. "You can do anything you put your mind to, just remember you learned that from me."

London, England
June 7, 1870

Percy woke after a restless night of tossing and turning. He had had another dream. He stretched and then, all at once, reality came rushing back to him in a wave of sorrow.

He was home, Father was dead, Charles inherited everything, and Rosemary was overcome with grief. He and Rosemary were left with nothing. Now Percy would never get to ask Father about becoming an artist. He would never know if Father would have approved.

After dressing, Percy strode into the corridor to find Rosemary gazing at a portrait of their family, painted nearly two years after their mother's passing. Their father was a handsome man; he wore a black suit and his shoes were polished to a shine, his top hat worn slightly at a tilt to match his jubilant smile. Percy, only six at the time, was grinning proudly. He wore a light cerulean suit and was holding a rose. Charles was ten; he stood in front of their father in a suit of navy blue, beaming.

Rosemary, barely two years old, wore a lacy pink dress. Her expression was of sleepy contentment as she rested in their father's arms.

"I miss him too, Rosey," Percy said softly as he walked up next to her.

She turned, surprised.

"Father loved us," Rosemary said. "I know that much."

Percy was silent.

Everything in the house seemed sad as if it were mourning the death of its master as much as the siblings were mourning the death of their father. The cheerful laughter that once filled the walls of Lancaster Manor was no more. They were on their own.

Chapter 5

A few weeks later …
London, England
June 25, 1870

Percy walked down the long halls of the house. The sun had barely begun to set. Suddenly, he stopped. The library door was slightly propped open and warm, golden light spilled from the cracks. Percy opened it slowly; the fireplace crackled mischievously amidst the bookshelves of the big room. Charles leaned over the wooden table in front of the fire, intently flipping through several papers.

"Charles?"

Charles inhaled sharply and slipped the papers into a large book. He turned and his gaze softened, "Ah, Percy! You startled me!"

"Should we attend the ball tonight?" Percy asked. "For Rosemary?"

"Of course, of course, Percy," Charles murmured in response.

Percy knocked softly on Rosemary's door.

He heard the gentle reply. "Come in."

Rosemary was sitting on her bed. She looked small and pale on the pink bedspread.

"I know," Percy began, "that things have been difficult recently. I was hoping it would lift your spirits if Charles and I took you to the

Midsummer's Ball tonight."

Her eyes danced. "The ball? Oh, Percy!"

Percy smiled.

The three siblings walked up the stairs that led to the grand building. Everyone, including the siblings, was decadently dressed. The stars twinkled overhead like someone had grabbed a handful of glitter and thrown it onto the large, black canvas of the sky.

The silhouettes of the twirling dancers in the ballroom could be seen through the windows all around the building. Percy looked at his sister. The glow had returned to her face; she grabbed his arm.

"We're almost there!" she said. "Come on!"

They entered the dazzling setting. The room was enveloped in a golden light that radiated among the dancing pairs. It felt right, the three of them together.

Percy's inner turmoil and restless spirit was almost forgotten as he watched Rosemary flit around the room like a butterfly just burst out of its chrysalis. He and Charles reminisced about old times. The candlelit room shimmered with the glow of peace and bliss. Rosemary danced all evening. She had just walked over to where Percy and Charles had been talking when a man in a black suit emerged from the crowd and approached them. As the man whispered something in Percy's ear, the color drained from Percy's face.

Rosemary looked between them, confused. "Percy, who is this gentleman?" she asked.

The man looked at her gravely. "Something has … happened." He gave a brief and solemn nod and disappeared into the crowd.

Percy's eyes darted back and forth between his siblings. He had to act quickly.

"Stay here, I'm going to get the carriage. We need to return home."

Charles rose from his seat and Rosemary nodded, her eyes wide with fear.

Percy hurried through the hallway to the entrance wondering how he should word the news. The whole family fortune—all of Charles's inheritance—was gone.

Chapter 6

They returned to the manor to find bobbies in every room. Rosemary hurried up to Charles. "What's going to happen to us?"

"Don't worry, Rosey, we're all trying to fix things."

His words were meant to comfort her, but his nervous tone only made her more concerned. Rosemary watched him walk away and went to find Percy. Who would have done this horrible thing? Who would have a motive to … no … she wouldn't go there.

The following morning …
London, England
June 26, 1870

"Rosemary, have you seen Charles?" It was Percy.

"He was in the library earlier, but I haven't seen him for a few hours. Can you not find him?"

Percy shook his head. He walked down the long hallway that led to Charles's room. The door was closed. Curious, Percy pushed it open. The hinges creaked to reveal ... nothing. Charles was not there, but stranger still was the fact that none of his belongings were either. The bedsheet was hastily flung over the bed, and the tables were bare and empty. Percy heard Rosemary come to stand at his side. She gasped and looked over at him, her eyes full of tears.

"How could he?"

Charles had left them. As much as it hurt Percy to say, it did make sense. That night in the library seemed suspicious. And Rosemary had said that Charles found the will, which strangely left everything to him. A forgery? He could hardly understand it; Charles had taken everything. It hurt Percy to think of his brother as an opportunist and a thief. He was the person Percy had always looked up to—but he would no more.

Epilogue

Charles stared out the window, his expressionless eyes tracing along the treetops ... waiting. Had it been worth it? He didn't know anymore. Would they forgive him after ... no, why hope? He was the bad guy now. There was no turning back.

Percy looked around; his head spun; the room spun. Poor Rosemary; all they had left was each other. He would figure out how to look after his sister as he always had. Percy shook his head. How could he have been so blind to the truth? How could he have trusted him?

Him. *Charles*. His brother. The person that he had trusted.

Line Breaks

*Tina Ramberg-Michael focused on **line breaks** in her revision of "Buttermilk Falls" with her poetry mentor, Tasslyn Magnusson.*

Dear Reader,

Poems are kind of exciting, right? Some of our normal "writing rules" of sentences and lines—*don't necessarily apply*. That's called "**Line Breaks**." When Tina and I met to revise her amazing poem, "Buttermilk Falls," we decided to look at how and when she broke lines and then, in turn, put lines into stanzas.

One of the best tools poets have to guide the reader through a poem are the line breaks. They control pacing, they control breath, and they contribute the tone in the poem.

There are two kinds of line breaks—*end-stop* and *enjambed*. End-stop means lines are a complete sentence or thought. In Tina's poem, here is an example of an end-stopped line:

Still scared of what I don't know, sometimes I write poems.

Rays bake my body and the stones,
Sunscreen laces my eyelashes and sweat stings my
tongue.

Still scared of what I don't know, sometimes I write poems.
That is a full sentence, and the line is complete.

A great example of enjambed lines is the final stanza:
I hold my breath
Air-tight, and
Plunge.

By making line breaks, Tina extends the drama of plunging into the waterfall by having the action extend across multiple lines. Notice how enjambment and end-stop both change the pace and feeling of the poem.

One of the first things we tried in revision was to remove all of the line breaks. To go even further, I suggested Tina remove punctuation! As Tina worked to put them back together, sometimes it felt right—the original line—and sometimes, there were new breaks and a different pace. As you revise poems, this is a fun way to explore your poem. Think about shape and space and story. Remember, a poem exists in the letters and in the space on the page.

Happy Writing!
Tasslyn Magnusson

As a fourth grader, Tasslyn Magnusson once tried to read her school library from A to Z, backward. She got stuck on P. L. Travers and Mary Poppins and has been reading anything and everything since. When she's not writing her poetry or working on her middle grade novels, she's reading fan fiction written by her teens and trading book recommendations with their friends. Tasslyn received her MFA in Writing for Children and Young Adults from Hamline University in January 2017. She has had several poems published and won the 2017 Room Magazine Poetry prize.

Tina Ramberg-Michael

– Author Interview

Tina Ramberg-Michael is an eighth grader living in the suburbs of Philadelphia. She plays cello in multiple orchestras, and loves volleyball and track deeply. Writing and English, however, are her true passions and she loves creating and learning—whether it's devouring some 2000's dystopian novel or penning her newest poem. She has no idea what her future will look like, but she's very much looking forward to it.

What changed as you revised your poem?

When I revised the poem, the rhythm of it changed. When I was more intentional with stanza and line breaks, it changed the rhyme placement and changed the pace of the poem. It made it sound more cohesive.

It was helpful to do this—it wasn't flowing the way I wanted it to—I didn't know what was missing until I did it, but once I fixed it I could immediately tell.

What can you tell other Young Inklings about line breaks?

They're more important than you think they are! When they're in the right place, you'll know. It's up to you, and it's about what you want your poem sound like—and line breaks are such a useful tool for that.

Where do you like to write?

I usually write in my room or in school. I do a lot of writing with particular teachers that like my poetry. I have a single document for all the poetry ideas. I might get two or three lines out, that poem might not work, but I can use those lines later. I have dozens of drafts I hate for one finished poem I'm proud of.

What advice do you have for Inklings who may not like revision?

It helps to remove yourself from the process. You're not really killing your darlings—you're just mercifully escorting them from the premises.

I love essay editing—you can take out whole paragraphs and make it so clear. The same is true for short stories. With those, I generally trust others' feedback more. Poetry editing is difficult, though. It's less technical and so personal, but not any less worthwhile.

Who do you enjoy sharing your poems and/or stories with?

With my parents and anyone who wants to listen to them! Sharing stories is such a good way to find and build and strengthen community.

What are you working on now?

I just finished writing a screenplay for a class. I wrote a few short stories—one was about AI and one was about a monster and a crazy aunt. Currently I don't know what I'm working on. This question might prompt me to start, though.

Buttermilk Falls

by Tina Ramberg-Michael

Buttermilk Falls

The hurricanes have nothing on this,
Its icy flow and plummet from the mountain side
While waters roar and collide.

Drowning itself a thousand times,
A buttermilk slaughter,
Falling
From the sky.

The end and the beginning sprawl before us,
Thunder in the ground; neverending movement.
Perpetually, interminably, magnificent.

Suddenly too small to mourn my newfound insignificance
I filter water through my hands, delighted by the light stealing me with it.
Drenched in the spray,

A temporary infinity, when my touch joins the cascade.

I forget to be amazed,
Quickly, naturally.
We trek back to the low ledge,
To the July water far too frigid but far too fragile to freeze.

I told myself I'd be new this year, learn to braid my hair.
Maybe start knitting again,
Start to change, to become someone I don't know yet.

I struck 10 years yesterday and I am so so young but can't know it,
I feel ancient.

Still scared of what I don't know, sometimes I write poems.
Rays bake my body and the stones,
Sunscreen laces my eyelashes and sweat stings my tongue.

I hold my breath
Air-tight, and
Plunge.

A Satisfying Ending

*Amaya Chugani worked through a final revision focused on a **satisfying ending** for her story, Faithful Birds, with her mentor, Rachel Delaney Craft.*

Dear Reader,

The ending of a story is one of the most important parts. It brings everything together, and it's the last bit the reader takes with them when they leave your fictional world. But the funny thing about building a **satisfying ending** is that it's not just about the ending itself. There are several things you can do in the beginning and middle of the story to set your ending up for success.

This is what Amaya and I explored while revising her story, *Faithful Birds*. Amaya worked on laying just the right number of clues throughout the story so that the ending would feel both inevitable and unexpected at the same time. She crafted a trail of breadcrumbs for readers to follow, except she used words instead of crumbs.

Amaya also delved into her story's themes. Themes—ideas like family, friendship, and loyalty—make the ending more powerful. They resonate with readers because they're universal, meaning we all have experienced them in some way. Amaya worked on bringing out these themes by developing her main character's relationship with her father and friends. She also did a great job of weaving birds into her story to create her own symbol of loyalty.

You can use these same techniques in your own story. When you've finished writing the ending, reread the story with fresh eyes. Ask yourself: *Did the ending make sense? Did it seem too obvious, or too confusing? What is it about?* Then you can tweak your clues and develop your themes leading up to the ending. Create a trail of breadcrumbs for your readers to follow.

When readers have a path to follow from the beginning, they'll enjoy the ending of a story even more—and it will stay with them longer after they turn the last page.

Happy writing,
Rachel Delaney Craft

Rachel Delaney Craft writes speculative fiction for children and teens. Her short stories have appeared in publications such as *Cricket, Ember, Uncharted,* and *Cast of Wonders,* and she edited the anthology, *Wild: Uncivilized Tales from Rocky Mountain Fiction Writers.* Her most recent novel won the Colorado Gold Rush Literary Award and was shortlisted in the Searchlight Writing for Children Awards. She lives and writes in Colorado with her partner, two dogs, and a succulent collection that is slowly taking over her house.

Amaya Chugani

– Author Interview

Amaya Chugani is a ten year old who lives in New York City. She enjoys participating in an Indian dance company and travels the world competing at dance competitions. Amaya spends her free time writing and reading. She uses writing to express her emotions. For example, she crafts poems and puts her thoughts and feelings onto the paper, while allowing her imagination to roam free.

What was the most useful or surprising thing you learned during the revision process?

I learned that waiting and being patient always helps. A lot of our writing is based on our real life, whether we realize it or not. So, if you take a break and focus on your real life, inspiration will come. There is no harm in waiting days or even weeks to get your mind off everything.

Do you think there's a little of yourself in your main character? How is she similar to you (or different)?

The main character in my story is Indian, like me. She is also very curious, and she is supported. Her friends are the friends I hope to have when I go to middle school next year: people who support and love me.

What are some of your favorite books or authors, and why?

My room is a library; it is overflowing with books, and this is due to my love of reading. If I had to choose: *My Family Divided* by Diane Guerrero. Guerrero explains deportation, detainment, and suicide, while telling the story of her life and struggles. I would choose *Odder* by Katherine Applegate because of the way Applegate plays around with the format and makes you laugh and cry at the same time. Lastly, either *The Hunger Games* by Suzanne Collins or *Orphan Island* by Laurel Snyder.

Are you working on a new story? What's it about?

I am working on a story called *Wind* about a girl's struggle to find her missing mother. She and her dad travel through the West Coast, both arguing and bonding, in search of her mother. This will be a story that will make you dream up the protagonist's triumph and laugh and cry.

Faithful Birds

by Amaya Chugani

The smell of *paratha* seeped upstairs as the sunlight that shone through my bedroom window woke me up. If you're wondering, *paratha* does have a smell. The sun reflected on the mirror as I changed into my clothes. It shone on my body like I was a star or something. I could imagine myself walking down a podium in a bright red dress. The spotlight sparkled in my eyes, and many people clapped and fans pestered me for my autograph.

My mom's footsteps snapped me out of my musings as she said, "Oh good, you are already dressed. I made *paratha*."

"I know, Mom. I can smell it all the way up here." I smiled at her and gestured for her to go down.

I brushed my teeth and quickly combed through my hair. I stared at my braces with such focus I thought my eyeballs might pop out. The new accessory made me self-conscious, but I tried to ignore it as I walked down the stairs for breakfast.

I dipped my hard *roti* into the cold *daal*. "It's delicious," I praised. I tried to make it look convincing, but I knew I failed at that attempt.

Mom looked away; she knew that I was lying. Her food had never been good.

"You don't have to eat it. Dad made *idlis* for snack and breakfast. He sent them yesterday. I'm pretty sure your father is trying to steal you away from me by cooking you delicious food." She said the last sentence with a hint of dislike, misrepresenting my father as an idiot and proving how she felt worthless in the cooking field.

I perked up at the mention of Dad's food, then tried to calm down. I didn't want to hurt Mom's feelings more than I already had. I missed my dad, and if it was not for his cooking (which is delicious), he might as well never have existed. I sighed. Life had changed so much since my parents got divorced.

Mom, ignoring my evident (or at least I thought it was) sadness, took the *idlis* out of the fridge and handed them to me. "Eat them on the bus, Inaya."

I nodded and ran out the door.

"Hey, Bianca," I greeted my best friend at the bus stop.

Some birds chirped and fluttered overhead as we immediately started talking. The bus pulled up in front of us. We quickly got on and continued our discussion. As I finished up homework, Bianca was telling me about where she wanted to go for lunch. I perked up at the mention of eating out for lunch (out-lunch), instead of eating in the dirty cafeteria.

"Hi, M." Bianca waved to our other bestie as Maiya got on the bus.

"We have to go for tacos," Bianca shared, droning on and on about her love for tacos. Me and Maiya stayed silent; everyone knew not to interrupt Bianca while she was on a tangent. We finally pulled up at school.

Later, I checked my watch to learn that it was 11:57, time for out-lunch; time had passed so fast. Bianca jumped up and down at the entrance to the school. I rolled my eyes at her childish behavior, although I was really excited myself. Bianca, Maiya, and I agreed we would eat at the Five Lamps for their famous weekly Taco Tuesday. I smiled at the thought of soon being stuffed with the delicious meat and tortilla crackers.

I checked my watch and gaped at the time. "We have a whole hour before we even have to start considering wrapping up."

Maiya nodded.

I giggled and smiled with pure excitement and anticipation.

"And you roll your eyes at me for being excited," Bianca retorted.

I gave her a thumbs-up to show her that she had made a good point. Maiya walked ahead into the restaurant.

As soon as Maiya closed the door to the restaurant, Bianca shouted, "On your mark, get set, go!"

We both raced ahead, swerving around each other, laughing the whole time.

"I wasn't prepared." I frowned playfully as I caught up to her.

She laughed and whispered, "Slowpoke."

We walked into the restaurant. Bianca slid down next to me and put her backpack beneath the table.

"I ordered chicken tacos for you, Inaya," Maiya acknowledged me and added, "And vegetarian tacos for you, B."

"Thanks," Bianca replied, satisfied.

"Yes!" I emphasized, knowing that if we buttered up to Maiya she would pay for lunch.

Maiya laughed at our obvious efforts and shook her head knowingly. "Never," I heard her mutter.

We continued talking as a girl from our school came up to us and said, "Hey girls! You sound like a bunch of birds chirping away."

We laughed at the comment and politely discussed it with her for a few minutes.

Then Bianca and Maiya started gossiping about Michael, the class troublemaker. I stared out the window, wondering what was happening in the cafeteria right now. Michael was probably being shouted at by Mr. T while some random song from the nineties that nobody knew played on the loudspeaker, I guessed, probably correct.

That is when the unthinkable happened.

I saw my dad wearing a Louis Vuitton bag and a Gucci sweatshirt. I gawked at him when he walked by, so shocked by his appearance that I didn't process that I had just seen my dad—who basically has no money after my parents got divorced—walk away in some of the most expensive brands in the world.

The divorce hit me. He had never even worn expensive clothes before he lost all of his money paying for citizenship. I was quickly overwhelmed by memories of the divorce and the work he put in to receive his citizenship. I felt a wave of sadness but shook it off. I couldn't cry here. The waiter coming to deliver our food snapped me out of my thoughts.

I quickly got up to chase my dad and told my friends, "I'll be back soon."

Bianca incessantly questioned me as I closed the door. I could practically hear her whispering, "Do you think she's okay?"

Maiya was probably assuring Bianca I was fine.

Outside, my eyes sharply moved at every fancy(ish)-looking outfit. I started giving up—fortunately not before seeing my dad cross the street.

"Hey, Dad!" I called.

His eyes widened when he realized who I was. Not with happiness like I had hoped but with fear. Not like he used to look at me when I walked out of my room with random scribbles all over a paper and he would applaud me, or how he would sit with me at the dinner table and we would act out my favorite TV show. He would smile.

He turned around and ran faster than I had ever seen anyone

run. I walked back to the restaurant slowly, contemplating what had just happened. *What was my poor dad doing wearing those expensive brands? Why was he running away?* I was overwhelmed with rivaling emotions, both confusion and sadness.

Back at the restaurant, I didn't touch my food for a long time, and I was so overwhelmed that I was not sure what emotion I presented. When Maiya asked how I was doing, I smiled weakly.

"Come on, get ready to go," Maiya told me.

She squeezed my hand, and the gesture said everything: *We are here for you.* She could definitely tell something was wrong. I took a quick bite of my taco and checked my watch.

As soon as we got to school, we changed for P.E. and quickly got onto the volleyball court. I dropped the ball three times, distracted by the flowing thoughts in my head. I didn't know what to do. All I knew was that I was hurting all over.

The day slowly passed. I went home. I didn't say a word to my mom despite her annoying protests. She knew something was wrong. I ignored her and muddled my way through the afternoon and evening, silent until I fell into my bed, exhausted.

It seemed like forever until the next day's out-lunch, the one time I hoped to get my mind off of yesterday's drama. At the local pizza restaurant, I bit down into the soft, gooey cheese as soon as somebody handed it to me. The tomato sauce dribbled through my mouth and the crust made a *crunch* sound so satisfying.

At least pizza never changes.

I heard a ping as someone walked through the door. Bianca and I kept on talking about the class election, but a jab on my arm told me Maiya had something urgent to tell me. When I turned to her, she gestured to the line by the counter.

I took in the figure she pointed at, its sharp blue eyes, its curved nose, and its jet black hair. I processed what Maiya was communicating. I blinked and stared at him once again: my dad! Two times in two days I had come across him. He sat down with some man in a blue suit and shades.

"I am going to the counter to get us some cookies so I can hear him better."

Maiya nodded, and then continued to listen to Bianca.

I heard Maiya laugh as I walked to the counter. I ordered some cookies for us. I strained my ears, hearing tidbits of their conversation.

"Having all this money" and "You haven't told anyone" and "We could make a great deal," the suit guy said to my dad.

Then my dad responded, "Meet me tomorrow at the Empire State Building at 12:30."

Their eyes were both so focused on each other, they didn't see me. They took the remainder of their pizza and walked off.

Yes! I can hear more at out-lunch tomorrow. And luckily, there is a great restaurant across from the Empire State Building.

I ran back to our table as my strategizing for tomorrow conquered my sadness about my dad. I asked my friends as soon as I sat down, "Can we go to the Articles tomorrow?" indicating the restaurant near the Empire State Building.

Bianca nodded eagerly, smiling at me in support.

We paid for our pizza and left the restaurant. I stared up at the sky, trying to notice the slight movement of the clouds. I bumped into someone, my bag clashing against theirs.

"Sorry," I muttered and ran ahead to catch up with my friends.

"Oh, there you are! We were starting to get worried."

I giggled at the inside joke. We walked ahead, and Bianca slung her arm across my shoulder. Maiya checked her watch and gasped.

I heard her whisper, "Two minutes!"

She ran ahead with Bianca and me at her heels. With every step I took, I thought about what I had just heard.

We made it to our Health and Wellness classroom, panting.

"You're late," Ms. R barked in her usual sharp and clipped voice.

We nodded, our faces full of fear. Ms. R was formidable in that way.

"Strike two." She continued with her lesson, leaving us in disbelief that we hadn't gotten punished.

Every single student in the classroom turned their heads and either gaped at us for not getting in trouble or gave us a thumbs up, congratulating our victory.

I sat down quickly and slung my tote bag over my chair. I folded my hands in my lap, pondering what punishment we would get if we got another strike. Last year, when the seventh graders got a strike three, they lost out-lunch. I shuddered at the consequence. I was so eager for Articles tomorrow, the last thing I needed was a third strike.

The day passed in a blur and I slept horribly because I couldn't get my dad out of my head. Was he mad at me for staying with Mom? Did he not want to be my dad anymore because he wasn't married to my mom?

The next day, when the bell announcing lunch time finally rang, I jumped to my senses. Not joking, I literally hopped, right in the middle of Ms. Sendila's sentence about our homework. Everyone laughed, but ignoring them I ran out of the room, dodging the people in the hallway.

Behind me, Ms. Sendila's voice rang out, "Inaya Argwal!"

I winced. "Sorry!" I shouted, praying she could hear me.

Luckily, I slipped away.

Later, I was staring intently at the menu in Articles, pondering what to eat. I kept looking out the window in sharp, quick glances, trying not to raise suspicion. In one glance, I saw my dad and "Suit Guy" walking down the street. They were talking about something, their faces painted with seriousness—for what reason, I hoped to find out soon.

"I'll be back," I let Maiya and Bianca know.

"Where are you going?" Maiya asked, a hint of accusation in her voice.

I winced at her tone, brainstorming some random excuse. I didn't want them to offer to come with me because that would raise suspicion (three tween girls spying on two grown men, not that I was planning on being noticed) and it would be rude if I rejected their offer. The two of them would also go crazy over anything they heard, even if it was my dad saying what he was going to eat for dinner. They would turn it into some big clue and come up with crazy theories about what it could mean. Bianca was gullible; but Maiya, she inspected everything.

Maiya's eyebrows raised judgmentally.

"I saw my cousin walk into a deli a few blocks away. I was planning to check to see if she was still there," I blurted out.

Maiya opened her mouth to address some flaw in my excuse, but then quickly closed it. To my utter surprise, she waved good-bye and nodded at Bianca to continue her story.

I walked away slowly, as if she was going to call me back. But she didn't. I picked up my pace as I crossed the street, not wanting to miss any of my dad's important conversation.

They had walked into the lobby of the building, and after a minute I walked in after them. I hid behind a group of people, who luckily were not loud enough that I couldn't hear my dad a few feet away.

Suit Guy whispered, "Remember this, you have more than five million dollars because of that theft we pulled off in June. The cops never caught us, and we stole more than twenty million bucks."

I gaped at what I was hearing. My dad was a thief.

"I know the whole story about your family. You think your wife is this scum, who kicked you out and divorced you and you will never forgive her. So you don't think they deserve any money, even though they're scraping for pennies."

At the scowl from my dad, Suit Guy added, "I agree, Max, I agree."

I growled quietly at what my dad had told Suit Guy.

"My proposition for you is that if you steal anything from that new exhibit in the MOMA on Friday, you will receive millions more."

Everything cut out for a little bit, but the last thing I heard was my dad confirming my worst fear by simply speaking three words: "I'll do it." As they walked out, I was surprised by my own stealth throughout these last few days. Though in seconds, my sadness and anger won over my astonishment.

I felt heavy throughout the remainder of lunch. Bianca noticed my sad expression and hugged me, and fortunately both my friends knew me well enough not to ask anything. From what I knew, I was the only non-complicit person who knew about this heist. A war formed in my head.

Should I tell someone?

Now you see, reader, I am talking about my dad here. He helped raise me; I have memories with him, positive ones. I was torn between betraying the dad I loved and staying silent, but I knew that keeping the secret would weigh on me every day.

Memories of my dad plagued me as I made my way through the day. In other words, to quote my favorite Charlie Puth song, "Memories follow me left and right." I suffered through countless reminders of the loving and supportive dad he was. I remembered how he would help me with my homework and remind me about multiplication tables. My favorite memory was how every afternoon when Mom dropped me home and then headed back to work, he would greet me by picking me up and twirling me around. I would laugh and laugh. How he kissed me on my cheek and then walked out the door with two suitcases, leaving me.

Thankfully, my friends knew that I needed to be with my own thoughts for a little bit, so when I was asked a question in class they whispered the answers to me.

I sighed as the bell rang, signaling the end of the day. Our science teacher, Mr. Kabe, called us by name to exit the room.

I practically ran out of the room as soon as I heard, "Inaya Argwal!"

I jumped with joy as I waited for Maiya and Bianca to be called. I was so relieved that school was over; I'd had enough pressure for one day. I had decided to sleep on the decision about whether or not I should tell somebody about what I'd heard today.

My dreams were filled with sweet memories of my dad and variations of what I had heard today, reminding me throughout the night of the decision I had to make. I woke up multiple times in my bed, sweating, panting, and tired.

Who am I loyal to?

Monsters tormented my dreams saying things like, "Your mother's scum. Everyone knows you are going to be, too. *Haha*! You're even scraping for money."

Then there would be times I would see my dad's face feeding me cake on my birthday. Sometimes I woke up crying. Sometimes I woke up panting. Every time I woke up, I checked the clock: 11:15, 12:00, 12:22, 12:46, 1:10, 1:19, 1:30, 1:36, 3:00, and so on.

My sweet, pleasurable memories popped up throughout the next day. During English, Ms. Sandipa warned me about daydreaming. I shivered at the possible consequences now that out-lunch was done. Ms. Sandipa smiled, satisfied that she had scared me enough. Then she started talking about the groups for book clubs. She went around the room asking each student what book they were reading.

When she called on me, I faltered. "Uh, uh. Wait, I know," I brainstormed, panicking, "*Odder?*"

The guess was obviously wrong, I assumed, due to the scowl on Ms. Sandipa's face. I winced.

"You are staying here for lunch," she barked.

I relaxed at the thought of getting some time to think things through.

After my (annoying) Advanced Algebra pop quiz, I headed to Ms. Sandipa's office for lunch. I flipped open my notebook to a blank page. I pretended to copy down some key points I remembered from class today while I actually jotted down the pros and cons of ratting my dad out to the authorities.

A weird fact about me: pro and con T-charts have been there for me during the hardest times of my life. When my parents got divorced, a T-chart helped me figure out who to stay with. The pros of ratting dad out were:

1. It was the right thing to do.
2. I wouldn't have to feel bad and overwhelmed anymore.

I thought back to the podium and my sparkly dress. Scribbling it down in the smallest handwriting, I wrote, *People might finally notice me because I will (hopefully) be on the news.*

The cons were simple: He was my dad.

Sadly, I left that lunch feeling more overwhelmed and confused than when I had entered.

When I sat down for dinner that night, my mom opened her mouth to say something and I immediately blurted out, "Dad is really rich and he got rich from a theft he committed and he is going to do another one and I overheard this in a pizza place and Suit Guy proposed an offer for another heist and he accepted and I have known for days and I don't know what to do."

Mom was silent for a moment. Then she handed me tissues, and I realized I was crying. I sobbed and sobbed while she held me.

"Now," she started in her soft, loving voice as she stroked my hair, "explain again, but slower."

"Dad is rich because he committed a horrible crime, and he is going to do another one soon for more money, and he thinks we're horrible people because ... you divorced him." I cringed at the last part, regretting saying it.

Mom just sighed. "You and I should go to the police station."

Twenty minutes later, I found myself sitting across from a young policewoman who looked very serious.

"So," she recapped, processing everything, "Max Argwal, your father, is going to commit a theft in the MOMA, tomorrow."

I nodded, too dumbfounded by my decision to speak. *I shouldn't have said anything.*

The next day, I woke up to the thought that they were going to arrest my dad and I was the reason. I started hyperventilating, in and out and in and out.

Stay calm. In and then out. In and then out. I grumbled under my breath as I checked the clock: 6:00 AM.

At lunch, I uncertainly told my friends, "Listen you guys, I overheard my dad agreeing to commit a theft. I told my mom and the police. Now, I am doubting my decision. Was it a good one?"

Bianca looked at me. "Of course it was. You did the right thing. You knew someone was going to do something bad and you stopped it. I get it, he was your dad. But still, you did the *right* thing and you shouldn't feel bad."

Maiya nodded enthusiastically.

Getting that reconfirmation warmed my heart.

I did the right thing, I thought.

I might not have my dad in my life anymore, but I had my mom and, thankfully, my friends.

Thank you to our Inner Circle donors. Your generous support makes the Inklings Book Contest possible year after year.

LA Biscay

Odette Harris

Kelly Hoy

Wayne and Anita Hoy

Aniket Kadkol

Ravi Kalkunte

Tracy Piombo

Eva Tsai

Wenjun Xu

The Yue Family

Thank you to our Collaborating Artists!

Julie Abe

John David Anderson

Kerry Aradhya

Kati Bartkowski

Rebecca Behrens

Ashley Herring Blake

Scott Bly

Dave Butler

Kacen Callender

Ernesto Cisneros

Kim Culbertson

Betty Culley

Jill Davis

Mandy Davis

Sharon M. Draper

Lisa Greenwald

Donna Barba Higuera

Marilyn Hilton

Joanna Ho

Ann Jacobus

Heidi Lang

Lea Lyon

Janae Marks

Beth McMullen

Patricia Newman

Daria Peoples

Mitali Perkins

Shannon Price

Helen Pyne

Caleb Smith

Laura Stegman

Raina Telgemeier

Ari Tison

Alder van Otterloo

Elizabeth Verdick

Ashley Walker

Pam Watts

Kristi Wright

Anne Young